SEX, MURDER & KILLER CUPCAKES

Sex, Murder & Killer Cupcakes is a work of fiction. Names, characters, places and incidents are the product of the author's imagination or are used fictitiously. Any resemblance to actual events, locales, or persons, living or dead, is entirely coincidental.

© 2014 Allison Janda

Published in the United States.

Join Allison on Facebook.com/AllisonJJanda
Follow her on Twitter @AllisonJanda
And visit AllisonJanda.com for excerpts, updates and more!

Your first book puts a lot of pressure on you to thank the right people. Whew, I'm already nervous.

A heartfelt gratitude to my mom for telling me I could do it, to Teri for being my most dedicated reader and cheerleader, and to Mark for not letting me delete the whole darn thing. Without the three of you, this book would certainly not exist.

I pretty much attribute my fascination with photographs to the fifth grade. The internet was fresh and Ms. Cunningham, my science teacher, was determined to educate our class using this new tool, despite knowing nothing about it herself. The assignment: research and write a report about your favorite animal. At the time, I had just returned from a vacation to Sea World and felt that my calling was to work with whales. You haven't lived until you're 11 and search for more information on blowholes. Suffice it to say, Ms. Cunningham was among the first to advocate for internet restrictions in schools.

My parents, both hippies who'd begun to lose their "copacetic" attitudes somewhere around the birth of my brother, were extremely protective parents. So protective that my dad, who never slept without a gun under his pillow, decided to earn his badge as soon as he found out my mother was pregnant with their first bouncing bundle of joy. It's only natural, then, that my brother and I were raised in a typical small-town Midwestern bubble made all the tighter when Ms. Cunningham called home that afternoon, on the verge of hysteria, tripping over herself with apologies. She was never able to make eye contact with my parents again.

My name is Marian Moyer. While I can't say that the experience in fifth grade scarred me, if you ask my parents the same questions, they would probably disagree. I will say that the experience turned me on, both literally and figuratively, to a whole new mindset. I became fascinated with photographs. I studied their every aspect — the light, the dark, the shadow, the subjects themselves. I poured over any photos that I could get my hands on, which included my older brother's porn collection, kept hidden in the back of his closet, behind the swell of hockey gear.

When I couldn't talk my parents into purchasing me a camera that Christmas, I drew instead, not wanting to forget a single detail of my surroundings. Trees, cars, people on the street — a modern day Picasso but with a rapidly growing chest. My mother, on the brink of madness with my constant doodling, finally gave in and purchased me a secondhand point-and-shoot in middle school.

In high school, I was still obsessed with my camera, learning film development and the art of catching just the right angle. Additionally, I was growing a mad obsession with everything related to food and (thanks to time spent in front of the television, eating my various creations) crime television.

By college, I was majoring in Criminal Investigation, minoring in Photography and working the cash register for a hole-in-the-wall bakery that turned out the most incredible doughnuts. My freshman 15 was more like the freshman 30. In addition to weight gain, I was also harboring a not-so-secret crush on a sophomore by the name of James Holden. Flattered, by which I mean creeped out, by my constant gawking while he worked his desk job in the student union, James finally asked me on a date. *Kabuki* was the most popular sushi restaurant in downtown Milwaukee. While I'd never tasted the stuff, I was well aware of what it looked like, having seen trays of it in the ready-to-go section in the grocery store. Combine its beautiful texture with my beautiful date and my mind was in overdrive with all the photographic opportunities that would present themselves.I tucked my incredibly out-of-date digital into my purse on my way out of my dorm room and have never regretted the decision.

While my camera was originally pointed at the crisp white plate, drizzled in rich dark sauces, I slowly found the lens following the line of James's lightly tanned hand, the curve of his muscular jaw line and the shadow of the light-colored 5 o'clock stubble that dotted his upper lip and chin.

Becoming aroused in a way that even my brother's porn collection had never produced, I found myself fighting the urge to remove my blouse and lie flat across the table, hoping my body would draw a similar reaction from James as the sushi did.

For the record, if you fast forward through the heavy awkwardness created by taking photos on a pity date, you're left hot, bothered and dateless in front of Dorm C. Still, I held in my hand a camera full of gorgeous photos that any food critic would be proud of. Well, food critics who could appreciate the art of outdated digital technology.

After some dramatic inner monologue which I won't bore you with, I decided that my idea of an underground publication focused on my love of both food and beautiful people was worth pursuit. Pushing James (but not the erotic reaction I'd had at dinner) from my mind, I threw myself into the creative process — all spare time and socially awkward experiences most suffer through in college sucked away. My best friend Addison tells me that it stunted my emotional growth (my first kiss came well after graduation) but it sure has led to a hell of a career path.

By my own sophomore year, more sexually frustrated than baseball fanatics' wives during a losing season, but 20 pounds lighter, I'd collected enough eye-popping photographs of various foods held by beautiful people around the city to begin my underground publication, *Foodtopia*, where food was never the lone subject of any photograph. And yes, my subjects were clothed. Hello, I was 19. By my junior year, I'd formed a bit of a cult following for the magazine which I slipped into copies of the student paper after hours. By the time I graduated, I'd decided that I wanted to let my inner freak flag fly with the publication and post it citywide, but wasn't quite sure how to manage it in that sweet, Midwestern girl kind of way.

Enter James Holden. Three years had passed and the only thing that hadn't changed was his magnetism. Fate, the saucy minx, had him waiting for coffee next door to the yoga studio I attended one afternoon. His dark, green eyes took in my bright spandex pants and slight flush from an overly vigorous power class — I never stood a chance.

Age had increased his charm, a gym membership had increased his bulk and I'm pretty sure that the dark roast he confessed to drinking religiously gave him some Amazonian jungle smell that can only be described as animalistic. Still, it was his eyes that captivated me the most: an emerald green; two raging storms of desire beneath his thick reddish-brown brows. A vanilla latte and 20 minutes later, he was nuzzling my collar bone while I was shimmying out of my yoga pants in the back of his Honda. Undeterred by the seat belt fastener digging into my back, the following 30 minutes served as my exit from studying porn magazines, trying to understand what all the fuss was about, and shoved me through the barriers to womanhood.

I never heard from James again after our fling. Stumbling from his backseat, however, I found that he'd again served as some kind of twisted muse. A few months later, I'd managed to turn *Foodtopia* — my fun, relaxed college-age publication — into *Food Porn*. It was still free and still turned out once a month, but now it was distributed throughout the city, featuring beautiful local models in barely (if any) clothing, posing with delicious handheld morsels.

So as to give it that sweet Midwestern spin, Addison,

who'd majored in Journalism, and I wrote up reviews of each bakery and restaurant we featured, making sure to sample as many of their dishes as they'd create for us. Doing so, we'd become both beloved and hated among the various chefs throughout Wisconsin and Illinois. The gig doesn't pay us much. Heck, it doesn't pay us anything other than in the form of new equipment. Addie and I keep it alive purely for the thrill. We do manage to offer meager stipends, college credits and some killer exposure for all of our employees, though.

While Addison's day job is reporting for a major local paper, I moonlight as a crime scene photographer, rounding out that crazy list of passions I've clutched to my heart since the age of 14.

In addition to being the talk of the food critic town, plenty has changed since college. Addison's fierce appearance has taken her far in uncovering some major scandals around the city. Something about being 5'10" and looking eerily similar to Cameron Diaz made people want to talk to her about things. Go figure. Meanwhile, her sharp brains have kept her ahead in the ever shrinking pool of what could be considered good reporting. She's a bit of a head case, that's part of her charm. While she's freelanced plenty outside the city, I'm convinced that Milwaukee will always be her home.

I remain a paltry 5'7" with pale skin, a bubble butt and insanely long auburn curls. I remain addicted to eating delicious food, reveling in real crime scenes and taking my photographs. While I'd like to tell you I outgrew that pesky fascination with dirty magazines, I own one in a sense, so I'd be lying. I'm still working to tame my insanely thick curls and figure out how an eyelash curler works, but unfortunately am still leading a much more boring personal life than all of my employment suggests. However, if I had known what was waiting for me, I think I would have embraced the boring and ordinary with far more relish, thanking my lucky stars that my twisted muse had left me to my own devices.

I knew that something was amiss the second I stepped into the studio. The morning had been overcast with a slight chill in the air, the smell of a late, damp autumn whistling through the few festive colored leaves that still clung to their branches. I clutched my coffee cup tightly with both hands, elbows tightly held to my sides as I pushed through the throng of commuters that clogged the sidewalk every weekday morning. I'd awoken late that day, hastily pulled my hair into a ponytail, scrubbed my face clean and raced out the door in the yoga clothes I'd fallen asleep in the night before. Not exactly my most professional attire and certainly not the best smelling, but it allowed me a much needed stop through the coffee shop and put our *Food Porn* shoot with some pastries from *Yummy Tummy* only ten minutes behind schedule. Or so I thought.

"Marian!" Addison yelped in surprise as I breezed into the studio, windblown flyaways giving me a somewhat Medusa quality. "Didn't you get my voicemail?" She paused. "Darling, we cancelled. I was getting ready to head into the Journal."

Numbed by the cold and not fully alert from caffeine, I paused, processing her words one at a time. After a few seconds, I started digging through my coat pockets for my phone which, coincidently, was dead, having never been plugged in the night before. "Perfect," I groused under my breath.

"Alec never showed up to makeup this morning and I didn't have the time to drum up a replacement," she informed me. "We'll have to have Betsy reschedule things."

As if on cue, Betsy, our short, adorable, freckle-nosed intern, scuttled into the studio, gripping her neon clipboard and speaking frantically into her headset. Her free hand pushed her silver wire frames back up her nose, but they just slid back down with every nod of her head. "Mmmhmm. Mmmhmm. Mmmmm. Mmmhmm. Okay, thank you," she said, clicking off and raising her gaze to meet ours. "Alec's roommate is in Tampa. He hasn't heard from Alec since last week."

"Damn it," Addison murmured under her breath. I caught the twitch that plagues her left eye when she's really pissed off. Betsy swallowed hard and her sweet brown eyes widened to the size of saucers. Addison had a famously short fuse. Upon reaching her breaking point, there was a nearly undetectable twitch of her left eye before she became a flailing, ferocious, red-faced string of cuss words, the tirade falling upon whoever stood closest. I slowly took a half step backwards, clutching my purse in fear.

Surprisingly however, Addison sucked in a deep breath, noisily releasing it as she closed her eyes, and shrugged her arms into the fall jacket she'd been clutching, cinching the sash tightly around her waist. This was new. And infinitely more disturbing.

I cut my gaze back to Betsy who was standing rigid, her clipboard clutched to her chest in a meager attempt at protection, eyes half closed, her short red bob offsetting her scrunched face, which had gone completely devoid of color. The cold, concrete studio was silent save for the echoes of Addison's deep breathing exercise. Betsy turned to me, her dark eyes troubled. I simply shrugged and shook my head.

After a few uncomfortable moments, Addison turned and began walking purposefully towards the stairs that led to our joint office. The clicking of her heels paused, the door clicked shut, and Betsy and I were once again enveloped in echoing silence. We released the breaths we'd been holding in a loud whoosh. I took a long swig of my well-creamed coffee while Betsy disappeared without a word around the corner, likely curling into the safety of her cubicle.

With slightly more bravado than I actually felt, I marched towards the stairs and up to the office ignoring the fact that my squeaky sneakers made me feel like a youth headed to the principal's office, after a failed attempt at rebellion.

Taking a deep breath, I knocked a little too hard on the door and let myself in without invitation. Being Addie's best friend, I was afforded the luxury of shoving my way into her life at times when most others would have been yelled at or cussed out. Her head was in her hands, elbows

15

akimbo on her beautiful mahogany desk, blond hair spilling in front of her ears. Her thin shoulders shook with the efforts produced by what sounded a lot like what I could only describe as lamaze breathing.

Clicking the door closed behind me, I cleared my throat to announce my presence and waited for her to speak. A few seconds later, the deep breathing paused. "My therapist said he wanted to recommend me to some anger management classes," Addison confessed between her hands.

"I hope you punched him."

Addison lifted her head and smiled, then thoughtfully began twirling a long strand of platinum hair around her index finger. "He told me that I need to learn how to manage my frustration properly."

I made a face and stuck out my tongue. "And you do that by working through the pain of childbirth?"

We grinned at each other before bursting into giggles. A few seconds later, her face crumpled and fell back into her hands. "What are we going to do about Alec?" she moaned.

"This is the third time in two months he hasn't called and hasn't shown up to a shoot. It's probably another hangover."

"We fire him," I replied simply.

"But he's gorgeous — our best looking male model," she stammered. "And that's saying something, considering that everyone who models for us has to look good naked. He doesn't even get paid!"

"He gets exposure," I reminded her. "And a lot images for his portfolio. *Yummy Tummy* paid well above what was necessary in order to be featured exclusively."

She sighed and spun around to face her window, which was just one story above street level. The trees outside covered the cloudy morning. You could almost be fooled into thinking that it was a bright autumn day if people weren't holding fast to their hoods and scarves as they pushed hard against the wind. "We're going to have to find somebody new. Can you ask Rory to throw together an open call?"

"I'm sure he'd love to hear it from you," I smiled.

She snapped herself around so quickly I thought she'd fall out of her chair. Stifling a laugh, I opened the door to let myself out. Despite Addison's on-again, off-again relationship with a model, Rory was madly in love with her. He refused to give up hope that one day she would succumb to his adoration. Taking the stairs down two at a time, Addison's angry howl sent goose bumps up my spine as I rushed towards the admin offices.

On the outside, our building was a boring, tiny warehouse with four single-square windows per side. It was situated in a quiet spot on Water Street, away from the hype of downtown. The main entrance consisted of two giant metal doors, which were heavily spray-painted, along with the rest of the outside.

Once inside, you were enveloped in a large, soft gray and white, albeit cold, concrete studio. Backgrounds of every

17

imagination hung from the ceiling on large black frames that could be flipped through like posters. Various lighting equipment was tucked into the cracks and crevices. A small pile of rugs and mats haphazardly took up a small corner by the door. About 15 feet away was a sturdy black metal staircase, which led to the only real office and a dressing room. The warehouse had once been a coffee-making factory. The faded, brown *Weise Butternut Coffee* logo had added some flair when we'd first moved in and not one of us had, had the heart to paint over it.

Just around the corner of the staircase was a tiny office, painted a blue as brilliant as the sky just before it tinges orange with sunset. The office was home to four paltry cubicles, two of which sit empty, each featuring a different theme based off of our well-known magazine covers. My favorite was the intern cube, featuring People Magazine's Sexiest Man Alive from a few years ago. He'd agreed to advertise Mootastic Chocolate Milk product and had needed an entire carton to cover his…erm…well, anyway.

When we were close to a deadline, the room — though small — hummed with activity and a lot of swear words. On days like today however, a full week after our release, the room is quiet. On the opposite side of my studio entry point, there are two regular-sized thin metal doors. One leads to our photo development room and my second "office" while the other is an employee entrance through the alleyway.

My second space is completely windowless, a former

warehouse storage area. I've charmed up my walls with various stills from the past several years and small boxes of photos spill onto workbenches, my desk (which is actually just three sawhorses glued together and stained) and even the floor. Strewing my coat over a wobbly stool, I set my coffee on a workbench, turned towards the cubes and scanned for Rory.

He's easy to spot, sporting a mop of thick sandy curls atop his 6'4" frame. While his suit coats never fit quite right and his glasses look like he pulled them straight from an '80s sitcom, he's of incredibly well-collected mind and vastly ahead of the creative curve. We can only afford to pay him a pathetic sum, compared to the amount of work he produces for us, but he inherited a ridiculous fortune from some great something or other and truly enjoys working in our humble space. No doubt you've seen his work in our publication. His layouts are award-winning.

As if I'd conjured him, the small metal door off the alleyway opened and Rory barreled in, nose tucked deep in his fully zipped store brand fleece. You'd never know the guy could buy Sweden simply by checking out his wardrobe. Out of breath and red-faced from the wind, he set his briefcase by the door and was slow to remove his jacket. "Hey kid, what's cooking?" he asks candidly in his British accent once he noticed my presence. Rory calls everyone "kid" despite the fact that we all, save for Betsy, are in our very late twenties. He told me once that he picked up the phrase from an American film and liked it so much that he decided to use it.

"That," I said, pointing to his beaten brown leather briefcase, "is foul and unnecessary." He smiled, bemused, and began walking towards his cubicle. Following, I asked, "Do you have time to throw together an open call for male models?"

His brow wrinkled in confusion and I could almost see his brain working through my words. "Didn't we just put one of those on this past spring?" he asked, hanging his coat from the old-fashioned standing coat rack he'd furnished his space with.

I shifted my gaze to the gray factory-order carpet, which had suddenly become incredibly interesting. Heaving a sigh, I kicked at something invisible on the ground. "He's not working out so well," I mumbled.

"Well that's too bad. Betsy is always telling me he's a... what's the term? A hottie with a body. That's it."

"Rory!" I reprimanded.

"I'm not the one saying it," he protested. "Besides, I certainly didn't think that he was the best candidate. But I was overruled." Giving me a pointed look, he sat down and swiveled towards his computer. I had to give him that one. The female staff members tended to get the final word on the male models. Addison, Betsy and myself would take turns choosing, as we each have drastically different tastes in men. Rory, being the only male in the office, was granted many more opportunities to pick and choose female models to his liking.

As his computer slowly clicked and whirred to life, he sighed. "I'll get something together by noon. Are you going to be around? Should I forward it to you?"

"Addie."

His back straightened considerably as he combed his fingers through his mess of curls. "Where?" he hissed.

"No, I meant forward the release to Addie," I corrected. His shoulders drooped and my heart ached for him. "But she said to tell you 'hi,'" I finished quickly, immediately feeling like a traitor. Still, this seemed to perk him up a bit and I slowly backed out of his cubicle and into the development room, allowing him to cling to the hope that "the model" (as I referred to Peter, Addison's boyfriend) would soon break her heart, leaving her open for a far more intimate office romance.

The only trouble with working in a windowless office is that you are never quite sure of the time. Stretching my arms high above my head, I took note of my growling stomach and decided I was in desperate need of a snack. No sooner had I thrown on my jacket, than there was a frantic, loud knock. Tripping over a bin overflowing with prints, I skipped the last few steps to my door and opened it with an annoyed "what?"

Betsy stood wide-eyed on the other side. She seemed to be practicing that look a lot today. "Addison said she needs to speak to you right away. It's an emergency."

"She's still here?" I grumbled, buttoning my coat and trailing after Betsy. "I thought she was headed into her

21

grown up job."

Upstairs, the door to the dressing room was slightly cracked and a light was on. Perhaps Alec had shown up after all. Opening the door to our office, I noticed that Addison wasn't at her desk. Craning my neck around the door, I took stock of my much disheveled partner, covered in a lapful of wet tissues, another pile gathered on a corner of her flawless, glossy conference table. Betsy darted around me and stood next to Addie, clutching a cell phone and looked incredibly uncomfortable.

Upon seeing me, Addison's chin began to tremble. "I've…been…texting youuuuuu," she howled, melting into a mass of tears and snot.

Closing the door, I gave Betsy a wary look before slowly making my way to Addie's side. I hadn't seen this colossal of a meltdown since Johnny Depp bowed out of a photo shoot due to last-minute scheduling conflicts two years ago. Nothing today had suggested that this would be waiting shortly before the lunch hour. No wonder Betsy had looked so agitated.

"It's…bad," she gasped, blowing her nose loudly. Fear clutched my heart as I waited for her to continue. Was it her parents? My parents? Peter? Sure her boyfriend was a nitwit, but I didn't wish ill on the man. Well, maybe sometimes, but now I'd feel bad.

"What happened?" I whispered, bracing myself for the worst. Betsy shuffled beside me.

Sniffling, Addison raised her eyes to meet mine. "Alec's

dead."

There was a beat followed by my loud nervous laughter. "What?" I asked, positive I hadn't heard right. "He's DEAD?"

She nodded and I turned to Betsy, sure that I was being Punked, but her face only served to chill me straight to my core. They weren't joking. "How do you know?" I asked, suddenly serious. My criminal investigation mind brushed off the cobwebs that had collected since college and clicked into high gear.

A look that I couldn't quite read passed between the two women. Addison began to weep again, softly, and Betsy motioned me out of the room. Out on the landing she turned to me. "She wouldn't let me call the police until you were here to tell us what to do."

Nothing was making sense and yet my brain was slowly piecing everything together, sending adrenaline coursing through my veins. Holding fast to the rail, I followed her to the dressing room. Still clutching her cell phone, Betsy used it to gently push the door open a little wider. There, slumped over in one of the chairs, was a very gray, lifeless Alec.

Having sufficiently heaved my morning coffee into a trashcan, I now sat slack and exhausted against the railing. Just because I make a living out of photographing crime scenes didn't mean I was prepared to see someone that I knew personally dead. Betsy stood over me, wringing her hands and chewing her lower lip with worry. "Should I call the police?" she asked in a small voice.

"What the hell kind of a question is that?" I barked. "Of COURSE you should call the police!" Pulling myself off the ground, I took long, shaky strides back to the main office and closed the door behind me. Sliding down to the floor, I covered my face with my hands. "You could have at least warned me."

Addison shrugged. "I thought that you of all people could stomach it."

Alec had only been with us for a few short months and they'd been tumultuous. It wasn't anything unusual for him to be late to a photo shoot or to altogether not show up, hungover from a night of parties, girls and whatever else 22 year old small-town boys enjoyed their first few years in a big city. Granted, I'd never wished him dead. Okay, maybe once or twice — but only when he was being difficult.

25

Still, I was far less disturbed by this news than say, hearing that my parents had been kidnapped by a Yeti. Or the small-town butcher who they both had an inherent dislike for. I'd never hear the end of that one. "I told you he was bad news!" my mother would shout at me in her thick Boston accent, shaking her angry fist.

"What now?" Addison asked me in her trembling voice. "You're the expert."

I shook my head to clear it and looked up into her sad, tired face. Suddenly feeling weary myself, my head lolled backward, coming to a rest on the door while my arms fell limply at my sides.

"Well...Betsy is calling the police." I shrugged. "We should wait here." I paused. "Did either of you touch him?"

She looked momentarily disgusted by the thought of putting her French manicure anywhere near a dead body. I couldn't really blame her. "I came upstairs to get my purse," she explained. "I saw we had some messages and decided to return a few calls before I left. Then Betsy came in and asked if we could close down the dressing room since Alec never showed." She took a deep breath. "I didn't even realize the lights had been left on from whenever he came in. He's never been here early; I didn't bother to check the dressing room this morning!" She threw her hands into the air in frustration. "I thought someone just left the office lights on last night," she sighed. "I thought that, that was weird and I wanted to make sure everything was okay, so I went to turn the lights off myself. I pushed

26

the door open and saw him. Betsy was behind me. No one touched anything other than the door." After a deep breath, she murmured, "It's just such a waste of...of...talent!" With that, she was doubled over into yet another tissue, wailing over the injustice of it all.

Moments later, there was a gentle knock on the door, which I tried to open, unsuccessfully, while still sitting on the floor. After several seconds of struggle, I cursed loudly then stood and yanked the door open, practically snarling at the person on the other side. Rory raised his hands in defense. "Betsy told me. I just wanted to check in with you both. See if you needed anything."

While a dear friend, in this particular instance, he was looking right through me. Still, I couldn't take it personally. I'd seen a lot of dead bodies throughout the last few years, some in much more gruesome states. Oh, and he wasn't madly in love with me. Stepping aside, I beckoned him into the office and quietly stepped out.

Betsy was leaning against the wall outside the dressing room, mumbling into her phone. Deciding to make a few calls of my own, I made my way downstairs to the front doors and heaved them open. They seemed so much heavier today. Crisp, cool air licked my face while tears I hadn't even realized were falling felt hardened against my warm skin. Swiping angrily at my face, I pulled out my phone, which was still dead. I wanted to throw the thing.

Soon after I heard the wailing of sirens off in the distance. Somewhat in a haze, I rubbed below my eyes with my jacket cuffs, then noisily wiped at my runny nose, numb from the cold. Chances are I'd recognize some of the faces. No point in being unrecognizable myself with a puffy face and red eyes.

It seemed like the whole of the Milwaukee PD descended upon the warehouse that morning. Cop car after cop car, vans, an ambulance, the coroner and even a fire truck. Our small staff huddled together in the studio, clutching the warm coffees Barry had fetched for us. Barry had been with the force for a few years but he never seemed to have grown out of being an eager young gun, constantly absorbing crime scenes like a sponge and forever fetching warm drinks on cool days when we worked a crime scene together. Today was a little different but suffice to say he never faltered, even as circumstances changed.

Somewhere in the middle of the same questions being asked by a different detective, I heard sharp voices just outside the main doors. There was a loud bang as one of the doors was wrenched open, then a deep voice shouted, "I just said you can't go in there!"

Peter's angry, twisted face appeared as he wrenched his way into the studio. "Pete!" Addison yelped, throwing herself into his arms. There was a flurry of embarrassing over-the-top passion, but it looked good on the pair, unlike how it might look for most other couples.

Turning away from the detective, I caught Rory's pained reaction, but when he met my eyes the pain was gone and an "aw shucks" look had replaced it. Walking over, hands deep in his pockets, he sighed heavily. "I hope calling him for her was the right thing."

Surprised, I turned. "You called him? Why?" He shrugged and I gave him a tiny smile. What a man.

"I left my shoot on the other side of town for this," Pete was telling Addison in his thick Chicago gangster-like tongue. His dark, angled features reminded me of an Italian mobster. "I'd better get to see the body."

Rolling my eyes at Rory, I turned back to the detective and continued to answer his questions, catching a crime scene photographer I'd seen many times before but had never actually spoken to scaling the stairs up to the dressing room. "That should be me," I muttered under my breath.

It was well into early evening by the time we were released for the day. Clutching business cards from various individuals "in case you remember anything," Addison, Rory and myself made our way onto the sidewalk, breathing in the clean, late day air. I'd spent hours at a crime scene before but had never felt quite so drained. Homicides sure were a lot more tiring when you were on the inside.

Peter, who had become disgruntled and bored after only a few minutes, left under the guise of needing to get back to the shoot he'd skipped out on. He'd called Addie about an hour later, inviting her to a party, which turned into an argument about his overall lack of sensitivity and her unwillingness to unwind. She'd hung up in an angry huff and declared that they were over! Forever! No one, save for Rory, had paid any heed. Peter would call back once he was drunk to apologize and the two would likely have mind-blowing make-up sex that night which I was sure to hear all about the following morning. I'd been privy to their break-ups and make-ups for many years.

The three of us shuffled uncomfortably on the sidewalk. I got the feeling that while none of us really felt like going home, we were all too embarrassed to admit it. Thankfully, Rory was the first to crumble. "Anyone need a drink?" he asked hopefully.

"Oh, thank goodness," Addison said. "Yes. Yes, please."

Linking elbows, we walked quickly towards the busier section of Water Street as it gained its pulsing, evening beat.

Eventually, we ducked into a small bar, decked out in Ireland's finest. Finding a cramped wooden table towards the back, we removed our coats before collapsing into our chairs, exhausted from the day. My stomach grumbled loudly, reminding me that I still had yet to eat anything.

Later that night, our pitcher empty and our bellies full, we walked one another to the door and parted ways after much hugging and promises to keep in touch throughout the week. Our studio was shut down for investigation and evidence collection for the foreseeable future. Over drinks that evening, Addison and I had decided to make a drive north in the morning, where we would stay with my parents for a few days. Rory was going to remain in the city and "hold down the fort" as he liked to call it.

My radio had been a welcome distraction on the slow drive home and I found that the deafening silence in my apartment left something to be desired. Even Fred, my red beta fish, didn't feel the need to make any relaxing swish sounds as he swam back and forth in his tank- the traitor.

Running my own business on top of freelancing for the MPD left me little time to care for a more active animal. There were times I photographed a crime scene so horrific that I would second guess my decision and troll PetFinder for a Doberman or a German Shepherd. Thus far, I'd never actually gone through with a purchase.

No matter what, I refused to be the first to break. I would not be the one who made the first call to the other two. It didn't matter how many times I closed my eyes and saw poor, dead Alec — with his graying face and cold, rigid fingers. I placed a hand over my mouth and swallowed the gag. "It's going to be fine," I told myself. "Classic mind over matter. Close your eyes and imagi- nope, don't close your eyes. Deep breath. Just think about something else. Anything. Else."

Trying to not think of something is pretty much impossible. In fact, it boils down to being the only thing you can think about. Nothing prepares you for finding a fellow employee dead. Moreover, you'll feel like someone has it out for you, even if it might not be the case. We'd pissed off a lot of people by writing poor reviews.

I double checked that both the knob and the deadbolt were securely locked on my door before digging for my phone which was, of course, still dead. Damn. The charger was in the bedroom. The bedroom had huge windows, practically begging for someone to break through them. Never mind that I lived on the ninth floor because that nonsense didn't matter when someone wanted you dead, right?

Fred had stopped drifting back and forth and had instead turned towards me with judgmental pause, his only movement the delicate fanning of his fins. "Fine," I hissed.

With great effort I managed to talk myself into turning on main lights, all the while keeping myself pressed close to the door, in case escape suddenly became necessary. When the apartment was awash in light with nothing amiss, I darted to my bedroom. Practically tearing my phone charger from its socket, I raced back to the safety of my soothing, sparsely furnished living room. Nothing could hide from me out here.

Building a nest of blankets and pillows, I collected Fred's tank, as well as a small, sharp knife from the kitchen and a king sized Reese's from the refrigerator. Cold dread was impacting my appetite. With Frank's tank balanced between my legs, I set about finding a non-CSI type show on my DVR (impossible by the way) and tore into my Reese's. Perhaps it was from the strain of trying too hard to keep my eyes open, or maybe the lull of Frank's oxygen pump, now plugged into the floor outlet by my couch, but I don't even remember falling asleep.

The next morning, well after rush hour had ceased, I made
my way across town to pick up Addison. I'd awoken with
Fred still resting safely between my thighs, knife gripped
tightly in my left hand and a line of chocolaty drool dried
to my face. Half of my hair was flat and half of my face had
been red with couch indentations. No wonder no one had
bothered with me during the night.

The sun glared hot through the window of my mid-size
sedan, which smelled like a combination of fear and
Subway sandwiches. Odd. I glanced around my car
quickly. A-ha. Real Subway sandwiches. I had two
wrapper-stuffed bags chilling on the floor of my back seat.

   The drive north to the small town my parents lived in
was going to be quick. It would be made quicker by the
fact that I was second guessing my decision to stay there.
Dead bodies didn't seem so terrifying in the daylight. The
Moyer residence, however, had been scary since the day
I'd started my publication.

   I don't remember my father ever having much of a filter,
but whatever decorum he clung to while raising us
definitely disappeared with his 50s. His motto had always
been to never leave things unsaid. When I was younger,
this saying mostly applied to boys I liked, boys I didn't and

35

things Addison would do to ruffle my feathers. Like the time when we were six and she shaved the hair off of all of my teddy bears, claiming she was giving them a haircut. What was left were three bald bears, with stuffing oozing out. Actually, come to think of it, the motto's application has remained fairly steady throughout the years.

While my dad's own brutal honesty was mainly directed at my mother's poor cooking, it occasionally spilled over into more uncomfortable topics, like his satisfaction with my mother after 30 years of marriage. I work in a pretty provocative line of business, but even I don't have the stomach to handle thinking about my parents dancing the horizontal polka.

Addison lived in a cute suburb of the city, her building filled with artsy young professionals looking super hip in their skinny jeans and beanie caps. I pulled over to the curb and threw the car in park just outside. I was reaching for my phone to call her when she suddenly materialized at the passenger door. Sliding in, she tossed a duffle bag in the back seat and perched her sunglasses atop her head. "Good morning!" she chirped in her singsong fashion.

"Good would have been after noon," I muttered, edging the car back onto the main road. "How long were you waiting downstairs? It's freezing out."

"Not long," she responded breezily. "But do you think we could grab some coffee before we hit the road? I could use a little pick-me-up."

"Late night?" I smirked. Pete was probably still asleep

naked upstairs.

She ignored my question, replacing her sunglasses to their rightful spot on her nose and turned to peer distractedly out the passenger window.

Two extra-large cups of coffee later, we were back on the road and headed north. While she and I talked about the magazine, the upcoming Ryan Gosling flick and even what hue she should paint her bedroom, neither of us touched on Alec or the fact that we had both gifted a considerable bonus to the electric company this month due to sleeping with our lights on last night.

About three hours later, I pulled up to my parents' brownstone situated on a nice little block just off of the interstate. My mother, who had called several times during the drive, said she'd have lunch waiting for us when we arrived. While probably not overly nutritious, it was bound to be more edible than whatever she'd throw together for dinner. No sooner had I killed the engine than the front door opened and 200 pounds of motherly spitfire stepped out. "I've been worried sick about you. I thought you'd get here much faster," she called to me from the porch, her thick accent giving away her Boston roots.

"We've been driving for three hours, Ma," I told her, stepping out of the car. "You called us six times." Opening the back door, I lugged my suitcase onto the sidewalk and began rolling it towards the house.

"Well, I was just worried," she reiterated, wiping her hands on her oversized sweatshirt before swiping them through her loose grays, eyes sparkling with an underlying fire. My mother was like a lioness. From a distance, she seemed completely sweet and controlled. You wanted to snuggle up in her lap. Once up close, it was too late to run away should she decide to go in for the kill.

"Hi," I said, rolling past her, pausing just long enough to exchange a quick kiss on the cheek.

Addison was hot on my heels but paused to give my mother a long, warm hug. "Thanks for having us, Lou."

Patting Addison on the back, my mother held the door open and ushered her inside. Before following us in, she glanced suspiciously around the neighborhood, checking for anyone who might have followed us.

"I can't believe what happened to that nice, young man," she said, shutting the door firmly once she was satisfied. "There's nowhere I'd rather have my baby during the investigation than right-" pause, big wet kiss on the cheek, "here," pause, big wet kiss on the other cheek. She turned and walked past us towards the kitchen. "I made up some sandwiches for lunch."

My father entered the hallway from his sitting room and took the liberty of putting me in a headlock and dragging me to the kitchen, much to my protest. Thankfully, Addison had been initiated into our family years ago when our families were neighbors. Her parents have since moved to a warmer climate, but Addie is always welcome back to our block with open arms. Most people that live on our street have lived here since Addison and I were small.

That's the way it is with tiny Midwestern towns.

After only a few seconds of trying to squeeze out of dad's iron grip, he let me go and gave me a bear hug, picking me up off the linoleum. "Good to see you kiddo," he whispered against my ear.

"Good to see you too, Pop," I whispered back, my breathing strained in his strong arms.

Dropping me back to the floor, he turned to Addison. "You too, young lady," he said, scooping her up.

"Don, let the poor girls relax, they're probably exhausted," my mother chided, busily stacking sandwiches onto a platter. My dad placed Addison back on the floor, then gave us a wink and edged quietly out of the kitchen, back to the safety of his sitting room.

Taking a seat at the kitchen table, Addie and I went back and forth in conversation with my mother who continued to slather various pieces of bread with mayonnaise before slapping a thick slice of meat of unknown origin on top. When the small talk and local gossip ran out, my mother proudly picked up the tray holding our lunch and placed it neatly in front of us.

My father took his place at the head of the table while my mother sat to his right. Addison and I both situated ourselves to his left. After a quick blessing, dad shook his napkin out and placed it in his lap. Hesitantly, he reached for a smaller hunk of bread and meat. Eyeing my mother suspiciously, he kept his voice level. "Looks like leftovers."

My mother's chest puffed with pride as she picked up the

platter and passed it across the table. "I made meatloaf for your father last night," she crowed. "He said he liked it."

"I said it wasn't bad," my father corrected, taking a bite.

Taking a few seconds to make sure he didn't begin foaming at the mouth, I took a small nibble of my own sandwich but stayed silent. My father, who'd grown up in small-town Wisconsin, experienced real life in the big city of Boston after graduating high school. He and my mother met in a bar, fell in love and decided on a married family life in the Midwest. They still dabbled in their hippie ways for a number of years after moving back to dad's tiny hometown, perhaps with greater vigor once they owned a home. Still, my brother's birth had, had a sobering effect. My own birth had wiped out any remaining desires.

Having served as a police officer himself for many years, my dad would no doubt want to delve into all the gory details of the reason behind our stay this week. Still, there was another matter of business that I suspected he'd want to address as well. Talking about his sexual satisfaction with my mother was one thing. Working in a business he referred to as "porn" and "for free" was an entirely different matter. It was a subject of contention that never stayed dormant, usually coming to a head over shared meals. When I was trapped. Like a rat.

"You know we're happy to have you," my mother said slowly, picking up her sandwich. "And if you ever need to talk…" she let the sentence trail off into the darkness.

"Here we go," I muttered to Addison under my breath.

My father, pulling on his poised cop face, took the opportunity to be frank. "Were you and that Alec kid knocking boots?"

Addie all but choked on her water.

"Don!" my mother scolded as her face reddened with embarrassment.

Ignoring her, my dad turned to face me. "Look honey," he started, putting his large, calloused hand over mine, dropping the cop face into one of fatherly concern. "It's not that your mother and I aren't proud of what you do. But the type of business you're in-" he faltered for a moment while my mother shifted uncomfortably in her chair. Clearing his throat he continued. "You just never really come visit us. We thought you might be upset because he was your...special...friend..." He coughed and shifted in his chair. "Jesus," he muttered and then, just as hastily, gave himself the sign of the cross as an act of contrition.

I felt my face getting hot with anger, over his stab at my work. "What do you mean the type of business that I'm in?" I asked, willing my voice to not quaver.

"Oh boy," Addie whispered under her breath. Leaning back in her chair, her arms crossed tightly against her chest, she gave my worried mother a Cheshire grin and waited for the fireworks. She'd seen my father and I argue many times. They weren't really arguments so much as short bursts of screaming followed by a door slamming (usually mine).

Sighing heavily, my dad shrugged at me, then took

another bite of his lunch. "Porn and stuff," he replied easily, through chews.

"I do not work in porn." My teeth were clenched so tightly that I could feel the veins in my neck bulging slightly.

"You photograph nude people," he raised his hands in defense. "I'm not trying to start anything, I'm just telling you how it looks from an outside perspective."

"From an outside perspective," I repeated.

Now he was getting angry. Even when my brother announced he'd gotten his high school sweetheart Rachel pregnant when they were both 18, my dad had remained calm and collected. His own little girl was an entirely different matter. I could see the smoke starting to steam out of his ears. "Yeah, to other people," he said through gritted teeth.

"Other people?" I was incredulous.

"How much did I spend on your education so that you could just repeat the things I said instead of forming your own words?" he exploded, standing up quickly and leaning over me, his face red and angry.

Pushing myself back from the table, I quickly leapt to my feet and stared him down before storming towards the hallway. "I do not work in porn!" I hollered over my shoulder.

"But the people are naked!" he roared back. "That makes it porn!"

"Not always!" I shouted back. "And when they are

naked, everything X-rated is covered by food!"

At a loss for words, he managed only an angry howl, cut off abruptly by the slamming of my childhood bedroom door.

I'm not sure how long I laid on the lacy white bedspread, clutching a bald teddy bear to my chest as I fought off angry tears. Fingering the stitches my mother had sewn to keep the stuffing intact, I went through the conversation again in my head. Sure my dad been concerned for my emotional well-being, thinking I'd lost my…lover. I involuntarily shuddered thinking of Alec and I together. Nonetheless, did dad have to link everything back to my magazine? Why couldn't he focus on the fact that I, too, had entered into public service, working crime scenes, my photographs helping to solve mysteries? For being a reformed hippie, he sure could be narrow-minded.

There was a soft knock on the door and my mother's head poked in. "Care to talk?" she asked in a way that suggested I didn't have much of a choice. While my father easily lost his cool with me, my mother was a rare breed, able to form all of her anger into "the look" which left her mind rational and thereby free for quiet, coherent conversation. In a way, it was far more frightening than my father. Frowning, I silently wished I'd inherited more genes from her side of the family, but moved over to make room for her on the bed. When I finally stirred up enough confidence to make eye contact, I was moved by the understanding reflecting from her eyes.

I sighed. "Ma, I-"

She raised her hand to silence me, then brushed my hair off my face and gave me a gentle kiss on the forehead. "He's just worried," she whispered, patting my hand vigorously. "He's been trying to make connections within the MPD all day. Seems they got a new Captain. Your friend Barry keeps trying to patch him through but it's not working."

"He could just ask me for those connections," I muttered. "I do work with the cops, too."

"He didn't want you to feel like he was checking up on you." Her long, hard stare suggested that, that's exactly what I would think he was doing.

"Maybe you're right," I groused, propping myself up on my elbow, still gripping my teddy bear tightly to my chest. "But why does every conversation eventually lead to the magazine? A few weeks ago on the phone, I was telling him about my trip to Chicago, which somehow turned into their underground drug cartels, which somehow turned into strippers with a drug problem, which eventually led to the publication." I shook my head, bewildered.

She shrugged. "You kids have made some choices he wouldn't have made for you." With a quick pinch to my cheek, she added, "But you're both adults. You live with your choices, not us." After a moment, she frowned. "I suppose we do put up with your brother's choices rather often."

My niece, Riley, was 12 and often rode her bike to the

warm comforts of grandma and grandpa's house when she was grounded. Just last year, my brother had cut down the large maple tree she used to climb out her bedroom window starting at just age nine. It was a mystery to us how she managed to sneak out now that it was gone and all that was between her and their front lawn was a long, hard drop. Riley put a shot of life into my parents' humdrum retired lives and, though they could both act annoyed and put out by her drama, they adored her.

There was another soft knock on the door before Addison poked her head in. "Lunch is getting cold." Grinning, she pushed the door wide open and motioned for us to follow her back to the kitchen. Standing, my mother turned to me, offering a hand to help me up.

When we returned, my father was silently chewing his food, holding a particularly large sandwich with both hands. Joining him, the three of us sat around the table. He looked at me and nodded once, his face normal in color. We finished the rest of our meal in comfortable silence.

The week at my parents' house had flown by. Being back
in my old room, within which my parents had changed
nothing, brought me a great feeling of comfort and safety.
Addison, who originally intended to stay in my brother's
room, often ended up camped on my hardwood floor,
cocooned tightly within layers of blankets. But despite our
childhood surroundings packed with nothing but happy
memories, both of us were unable to sleep much. It seemed
that every time we tried, we were startled back to
consciousness by Alec's body lifeless behind our eyelids.
Eventually, we would be pulled into slumber by pure
exhaustion, the other's soothing breath, or both.
We treated my parents to breakfast every morning, a
surprise that had my father giddy with anticipation every
time he awoke to something other than the usual smell of
burning bacon and watered down coffee.

   I'd spent plenty of quality time with Riley, Rachel and
my brother, John — as often as was allowed, which was
pretty often. Addison and I had helped rake their lawn and
finished up various projects around their house. We
finished our days lazily blowing bubbles from the porch
swing or pointing out various shapes in the clouds as cool
afternoons faded softly into crisper autumn evenings.

Nothing can snap me into a reverie like the change of seasons, which was far more noticeable out in the country than back home in the suburbs.

Barry had called me a few days into our escape and informed me that we'd be allowed back into our offices by week's end. The autopsy hadn't turned up anything unusual he said, but they were still waiting on the toxicology report, which was known to take a bit longer. Thankfully he promised me, with a little too much enthusiasm, homicide had been ruled out, meaning that we'd be safe upon our return, for sure. My thoughts turned briefly to Fred, who I now knew was safely swimming about his bowl, waiting for me to come home. I'd had a horrible dream the night before that I returned to a ransacked apartment, Fred's bowl broken into shards that were scattered across my floor. Sentimental for a fish? Perhaps. But while I'd managed to kill just about every plant that had entered my apartment — including a cactus — Fred was nearly seven and still going strong.

Before we hung up, I made Barry swear to remove the chair that Alec had been sitting in, not wanting to have to do it myself. He laughed but promised to take care of it.

Sunday evening following dinner, which had also been attended by my brother and his family, my mother handed Addison and I each a paper sack filled with leftovers. The spaghetti, while chewy, hadn't been her worst endeavor in the kitchen and the berry crisp, which Rachel had prepared, was absolute heaven. After hugs, kisses and multiple goodbyes, Addison and I hopped into my car and drove back to the city. Neither of us spoke as we sped past dark, empty fields on the unlit stretch of highway, but sad songs played on every FM radio station all the way home.

Dropping her off at her apartment, I waved and waited for her to get all the way inside the secured entrance before I pulled away from the curb. We'd conference called Rory and Betsy a few minutes before we reached town to fill them in on Barry's report and we had all agreed to meet at the warehouse at seven in the morning, before venturing inside together. While Rory and Betsy were the only ones who had any real work to do there tomorrow, Addison and I weren't about to let them go in alone.

I awoke to another gray dawn, cold rain giving my windows a warped appearance. The apartment had been exactly as I'd left it just a week ago and yet, things weren't quite the same. My suitcase sat unpacked by the front door and my empty leftover cartons from my parents' house lay open on the floor in front of where I'd fallen asleep on the couch. Rubbing the sleep from my eyes, I reached for my phone and clicked off the alarm, then lay back into my pillows, waiting for that tiny burst of willpower that would get me upright.

Following a long, steamy shower, I hastily tidied up my apartment, fed Fred and locked up. Checking my watch, I decided that the stairs would be much quicker than the elevator and walked quickly towards the emergency exit signs which glowed eerily. I was in such a rush to get to my

car that when I went to pull my keys from my purse, I
stumbled right into the man in front of me who was
squatting to pick up something he had dropped. As soon as
I bumped into him, he pitched forward but managed to
catch himself and spin quickly, helping me to regain my
own balance. Still somewhat caught off guard, I glanced up
to thank him and realized that I was staring right into the
gorgeous green eyes of James Holden.

I felt my face flush instantly and my hands immediately
went to smooth my blouse, which I instantly wished was
just a bit sexier. "James!" I stammered in surprise. "How
have you been?"

"Marian Moyer," he replied with an easy smile. "It has
been a long time."

"Six years." The words flew out of my mouth and I
immediately clapped my hand over it. Idiot.

He laughed, but not in a cruel way, then stuffed a hand
into his coat pocket. "I guess that, that makes sense."

There was an awkward silence so I shifted my gaze to my
feet and pulled my handbag up on my shoulder. I felt the
blush burning strong on my ears and neck. Fiddling with
my keys for a moment, I cleared my throat and tried to
think of something intelligent to say. When nothing came
to me and when he didn't say anything further, I mumbled,
"Great to see you," then stepped around him and quickly
walked towards my car.

"Marian," he called after me. Pausing but not turning
around, I waited. "Have dinner with me. This Friday." I

could hear the smile in his next sentence. "How about *Kabuki*, for old times' sake?" I turned to face him, stunned, but managed to give a curt nod of approval. "Great," he answered. "Meet you there at six?" With a flick of his wrist, he tossed his keys up into the air, caught them, gave me a sly smile and then walked the opposite direction.

I was on Cloud 9 my entire drive. My normal road rage didn't even kick in when I got cut off as I approached my exit. As I slowly rolled past the entrance to our warehouse, I noted that the other three were already there, hoods pulled tightly to their heads to shield them from the cool drizzle. Parking behind the building on the pebbly lot, I grabbed an umbrella from the back seat and hurried towards the front.

"We've been waiting forever!" Addison cried as I scurried up the driveway.

"Five minutes," I replied. Once closer, I cast her a sideways glance. She caught the glint in my eye and her face lit up, her eyes telling me she knew exactly what I was communicating. "James?" she mouthed as Rory, oblivious, unlocked the door to the warehouse. She knew that he was the only man capable of putting me into such a giddy state. Rory holding the door for us, Betsy marched her way inside first, followed by me, then Addison who was clutching my shoulders and gently shaking them with pure glee. Rory pulled up the rear. Before the door closed, he flipped the light switch and our studio was awash with soft lighting. All signs of muddy shoe debris that had been trailed in by the string of law enforcement, all the sticky dust that was used to check for fingerprints were gone. Barry had sent a service in to clean up the scene after they'd finished, "to be billed to the department," he'd told me over the phone when he called to inform me about the autopsy results — the pride in his voice clear. As we shifted our gaze higher, we noticed that both the door to the main office and the dressing room door hung wide open.

Addison reached out to grab my hand and the two of us slowly crept towards the staircase with the other two trailing close behind. Together, we slowly made our way to the upper landing. We glanced first into the main office, which had been left untouched. In fact, nothing had changed other than that the message light was flashing an angry red 13. Pausing, we backed out and glanced at the other door, which waited inviting and open just a few feet away. Addison tossed her hair and took a deep breath, then crossed the divide and flipped the light on. It, too, gave no indication that anything had been amiss only about a week before. As promised, Barry had removed the chair and the room stood completely bare save for the lighting around the mirrors playing off the soft green walls.

"I'll order a new chair today," Rory said quickly. We all mumbled our thanks, then flipped off the lights, closing the door behind us. Trooping slowly down the stairs, our footsteps echoed eerily throughout the studio.

Back at the entrance, Addison and I waved our

goodbyes, making Betsy promise to call us if anything was amiss. Rory wrapped an arm around Betsy's shoulder, then gently pushed her behind him before she could share what was clearly on her mind. "There won't be any issues," he promised, fixing her with a look. Then turning back to Addison he said, "Remember the call is set for tomorrow morning at ten."

Addison smacked her forehead. "Bob is going to kill me," she moaned. "I can't believe I already blanked that."

"You've had an eventful week," he shrugged. "See you tomorrow." With that, he shooed us out and closed the door.

Walking towards our cars, tucked under the security of my umbrella, I turned to her. "Bob isn't happy with all the requests off?" I asked, sympathetically. While being a freelance crime scene photographer definitely had some downsides, the one thing I could always count on was free time as I found myself needing it.

"No," she mumbled. "He asked me to write the story on it all before I left town last week, but I told him, 'no way.' "

I nodded sympathetically. "Too close to home?"

"I just wouldn't be able to look at it from the perspective of a journalist," she admitted. After a brief pause she raised her fist to the air and shook it before saying in a deep voice "A good journalist can write anything!"

I laughed. "Does your boss know what a great impression you can do of him?" Bob, who reminded me of J. Jonah Jameson from the Spiderman comics, was loud, impersonal and always forgot who I was.

She smiled at me briefly and then, suddenly remembering our earlier exchange, her eyes grew wide with anticipation. "So?" she squealed. "Tell me what happened with you this morning!"

We had reached our cars but I took a second to fill her in on my extremely ill-prepared run-in with James. I finished and grinned widely, completely unable to contain my elation over my upcoming date at the end of the week, but Addison's face had turned from excitement to a look of motherly compassion just before delivering bad news. "You'll be careful, right?" she asked me, searching my face. "You know how that ended last time."

I frowned. "It was a long time ago," I countered. "And I've dated since then. I know what I'm doing now."

Addison snorted. "I've dated much longer than you have and most days I still don't know what I'm doing."

"Oh, please. You and Pete already made up. He was still upstairs when I came to pick you up the other morning," I chided. "You know exactly what you're doing."

She ignored my comment. "You've already slept with James once, so you don't have to worry about anything related to that."

I reddened. "That was a long time ago, too."

She shrugged. "It won't have changed much. Other than the fact that you've gained a little more experience." She paused, then with a wicked grin said, "And have a much more delicate palate than the back of a Honda outside a coffee shop."

"Go to work," I retorted, pretending to be offended. She laughed easily and gave me a gentle shove, then pulled me in for a hug. "See you tomorrow," she said. Then with a wink, she climbed into her car. I waited until her door was closed before I moved the umbrella and started walking back towards my own vehicle.

The only thing on my agenda today was to tackle household tasks that included grocery shopping and a lot of laundry. The whole bit sounded incredibly boring and domesticated — neither of which I was feeling in that particular moment, revved up by memories of sleeping with James. Once inside my car, I started the engine, then pulled out my phone to check my bank account. "Not much but just enough," I smiled. A few minutes later, I was headed west towards the mall, hoping to find just the right outfit for my date later that week.

I hadn't dated much in the last few years. There was one semi-serious relationship but no one that ever really moved me long-term. I seemed to draw in a lot of nutcases, probably due to my line of business. While I'm a naïve, Midwestern girl at heart, something about taking almost-nude photographs of really attractive people followed by an afternoon clicking away at the scene of a homicide doesn't exactly suggest that to potential suitors. Actually, when I put it like that, it makes a lot of sense. Still, even though James had been a heartless bastard for stealing my virginity and never calling, something inside me never quite let go of the hope that somewhere down the road things would work out for us. It was complete romantic doe-eyed nonsense, but fate did seem to have a way of repeatedly bringing us back together, despite the very different lives we likely led. I found myself wondering what he did these days, why we'd run into one another outside the apartment and if he still drove his beat up Honda.

It's funny to look back at that exact moment in time, simply because I was beside myself with excitement. I had no idea what a horrific chain of events would follow that single run-in, in my parking lot. However given past experiences, I probably should have guessed.

I stretched noisily in my metal chair, then reached for my coffee with a yawn. The previous day in the middle of my shopping expedition, I'd gotten a call asking if I was free to photograph a homicide. While it wasn't at the top of my list of things I wanted to do at the moment, my mind still ripe with Alec's death, my bank account disagreed and I found myself among what remained of a love triangle gone terribly wrong.

Crime scene photographs, unlike the photos I took for the magazine, are incredibly complex. In cases where a crime goes to court, a photo of the aftermath can say a thousand words. However, it must meet very specific requirements to be entered as evidence. The hardest part for me was always flipping the emotional switch in my brain and shooting things from a technical perspective. It wasn't my job to choose a side, it was my job to record the evidence.

The shift had run late into the day and various standing and squatting positions had all but exhausted my legs. By the time I stumbled into my apartment, I'd only been able to manage a hot bath and bed, my microwave meal from the night before thawed out but uncooked on my kitchen counter the next morning. I'd barely had time to stop for coffee before stumbling into the studio only seconds ahead of our scheduled call.

We were taking a short break in between our next round of models. While our subjects ultimately did have to strip down to just their undergarments, we first spoke with them about their background, their accomplishments thus far and ultimately their goals. A vibrant personality could go far in swaying our opinion. Meanwhile, those who didn't impress us while clothed rarely saw an opportunity to show off their bodies.

The original call had been for male models but Rory had "mistakenly" input a need for females as well. "They don't get paid anyway," he argued. "We may as well build up our cache." Thus far, we'd been unimpressed with what had come through our doors. Still, we had a few hours yet ahead of us and we were bound to find at least one diamond in the rough. The Midwest isn't exactly crawling with the same daily vibrancy as say, L.A. or New York, but you'd be surprised at what could walk in our doors. We might have been a free publication but we had a name and a reputation.

"Are you ready for our next guest?" Betsy called out from behind the black curtain we'd erected in the studio. It blocked both our chairs and our makeshift set from those who were waiting to be seen.

Rory eyed Addison and I for the go-ahead. When we both nodded in approval, he shouted, "Send 'em in!"

Betsy stepped out from behind the curtain and made her way to the stool which sat pooled in soft light upon our makeshift stage. Once she was seated, she smoothed her skirt and gave the three of us a smile.

"Betsy, I meant send in the next model," Rory reprimanded frowning and looking back down at his notes.

"I am the next model," she replied. The three of us just stared at her as if she had suddenly sprouted three heads. "Hear me out!" she pled, noticing our confusion. "When I originally came to you, I'd wanted an opportunity to model but you weren't looking for someone new, so I agreed to the internship."

"Betsy," I said gently, "we're still not looking for female models. That was just a mistake." Rory guffawed loudly and I shot him a look. Turning back to Betsy I added, "Please send in the next MALE candidate. Okay?"

"But Rory just said!" she shouted, practically in tears. "I heard him! You don't pay the models anyway and there's nothing wrong with adding someone new to the list if they have potential. I have serious potential. I just know I do."

I fixed Rory with another look, but he ignored me, his gaze remaining fixed on his notes. I wanted to stab him with my pen. Desperately, I eyed Addison for backup.

"Betsy, we don't have a need for female models right now," she said firmly. "We haven't brought any new women on board today and we've seen-" she scanned her list briefly, "over a hundred. We told every single one no."

"Speak for yourself," Rory muttered.

"You're no better than any of the other young ladies that have come through, and certainly no worse, but we still don't have use for you as a model right now," Addison continued. "You're a decent intern. Stick with that this semester and please send in our next applicant," Addison admonished. There was no room for discussion in her voice.

"But-"

"Now," Addison cut her off, glancing back down at her pile of papers. "I won't ask again."

Betsy climbed, distraught, from her stool and made her way slowly back behind the black curtain. A few moments later, we heard footsteps approaching the set. Though I hadn't turned to look, I felt as if all of the air had been sucked out of the room while my hair practically stood on end with electricity.

Once he'd walked into our line of vision, I felt myself suck in a deep breath. Not a single bit of him was what I was expecting and yet, he looked so incredibly familiar. His skin was olive in tone and his hair was a wavy brown. However, it wasn't his lean physique and tall stature that drew you to him, it was his eyes. They were the same color you'd see viewing sunlight from below the ocean surface — the brightest blue.

Sitting motionless, I realized my mouth was hanging open. Clamping it shut quickly, I glanced both left and right to view the others' reactions. Even Rory seemed stunned by our sudden stroke of luck. "Your name?" he finally uttered, glancing down at his call sheet.

Startled by the break in silence, I dropped my pencil and

fumbled around for it momentarily before moving back to my chair and letting out a small embarrassed laugh, which was more of a honk. Blushing, I ducked my head and furiously pretended to be writing very important things.

"Mikael," he replied in a soft lilt that I couldn't quite catch. "But everyone just calls me Mika." He brushed a wave off his forehead and beamed. His smile had a slight crookedness that only served to increase his attractiveness, causing me to nearly fall out of my chair. Or maybe that last bit was caused by his dimples, it's hard to say.

"I see," Rory responded, a little too impressed for having only heard a name. "And Mika, tell us a little about yourself."

"Well…" he started hesitantly, shifting on his stool. "My mother is Finnish and my father is from the Ukraine. We moved to New York when I was 15."

"And how long ago was that?" Addison asked, shooting me a wink. God love her.

"Are you allowed to ask that?" he asked with a good-natured laugh. The sound was melodic. He had fire. I liked it. I liked it a lot.

We all giggled back. Even Rory, which was even more funny, causing Addison and I to laugh harder. "No," she responded, "but it's off the record."

"Personal curiosity," Rory added dryly, wiping the mirth from his face.

"About 15 years ago," Mika told us with a smile.

I sank back in my chair with relief. I never quite got over

feeling old when I found younger male models attractive. There were a lot of them. It seemed like no one in the industry was much past the age of 25. "Anyway," Mika continued. "I followed a girl to Milwaukee." My heart sank in disappointment and I felt charged with an irrational jealousy. "But that didn't work out," he continued quickly as I felt myself perk up again. "I guess I just decided to stay."

Rory noticed my emotional investment and rolled his eyes. Mika's hold had clearly worn off for him.

"I've worked in carpentry my whole life," Mika added, folding his hands in his lap.

"Carpentry," I murmured surprised, shifting my gaze to his hands, which didn't look worn at all, but incredibly smooth. "Why are you here, then?" I asked.

"Not that she's complaining, you see," Rory added and I wished silently, again, that I could stab him in the neck with my pen.

Mika seemed to give this some thought but shrugged, seeming to come up empty. "I'm not sure," he admitted. "I still love working with my hands. My father taught me the discipline. But I saw an ad for this and I just thought I'd… check." He looked down at his feet and shook his head. "Silly right?" he asked us, pushing himself off the stool. "No experience and here I am, trying to get a gig at a place like this. I'm sorry I wasted your time."

"No!" the three of us cried in unison, shooting out our arms to stop him.

Mika looked momentarily stunned but sat back down, gripping the stool tightly with both hands.

"It's just-" Addison started. She paused and licked her lips, then glanced at Rory for help as I was clearly rendered useless verbally.

"It's true that we feature a lot of big names," Rory chimed in. "But save for the occasional small fees we're granted from ads and feature stories, we don't collect."

"We don't pay our models" I added, finding my voice. "So if you're looking to totally switch careers, we might not be the best place to start." I hated myself even as I said it. What 30 year old could afford to not only totally change careers, but also take gigs that were unpaid?

"Oh, I'm not looking to get paid," Mika said horrified. "I still plan to work outside of this. Will I not have the time? Did I give the impression of needing a paycheck?"

Addison giggled. "Of course not." She seemed to consider something for a moment, then asked, "How many languages do you speak?"

Looking somewhat embarrassed, Mika switched his gaze back to his feet. "Five," he told us. "Ukrainian, Russian, Finnish, Swedish and English."

"That's quite the resume," Rory said, once again impressed by our luck. "There are some really well-paid jobs where you could put those skills to better use. Even better than carpentry or modeling." Addison and I shot him daggered looks. "What?" he hissed at us, shrugging. "There are!

63

Mika smiled. "I guess I just prefer," he searched for the right words, then added, "doing my own thing."

"Well, he's got my vote," Addison said, tipping back in her chair and chewing the end of her pencil. "Which is just as well because getting back to my grown up job early will score me good favor. I hate it when the boss is mad. He'll still assign me crappy stories."

"You've been nominated for Journalism awards," Rory told her, incredulous. "And he'll still assign you to the Mom and Pop shop feature article?"

"He's a very vindictive man," Addison assured us.

"Excuse me," Mika asked, quietly. "Does this mean that I have it?" His voice was low and warm.

"Yes," Addison grinned. "And one more thing before you go," she added, raising a finger. Grinning devilishly at me, she continued. I could feel a full body blush starting at my face, blanketing my neck and slowly prickling its way down my arms and legs. "Given the nature of the publication, I'm going to need to ask you to remove your shirt and pants, please. It's strictly professional, of course."

"Oh, of course." He complied, albeit with more confidence than I would have predicted, given his humble roots. I managed to push the thought from my mind as soon as he'd removed his shirt. Oh, baby!

Later that afternoon, I was working quietly in the upstairs office. Addison left almost immediately after we sent the remaining models home and I gave Betsy the afternoon off to sulk, though that's not exactly how I phrased it when I told her to take a hike. Rory usually checked in before leaving, but it was possible that he was sulking also. While he knew that Mika was no doubt the right decision, Addison had always dated models and our latest threw a wrench in his plans now that Pete and Addison had ended things. Or were they back on again since our return? She never did confirm that he'd been in her apartment the day I picked her up to head north. Really, though, who could keep track?

"You seemed interested," Rory had said to me pleadingly as he followed me up to the office earlier that day. "Just ask him out before she does."

"Ha!" I'd responded. "I'd be surprised if she hasn't asked him out already."

The office phone rang loudly and I jumped, startled by the break in silence. I'd almost been ready to pack up and call it a day but I didn't want to miss out on anyone hoping for an exclusive, so I cleared my throat and picked up on the third ring. "Hello, this is Marian," I found myself

65

saying, "how can I help you?" The other end of the line was quiet, save for someone breathing softly and a few quiet crackles. I waited for a beat. "Hello?" I asked again. More breathing. More crackles. I felt the hairs on the back of my neck start to prickle and I clutched the phone so tightly that my knuckles went white. "Look," I said firmly. "If this is-"

"Marian? Marian?" a voice cut through, but faded back out quickly.

"Barry?" I asked, surprised.

"I'm on the- I'll call you- one? -ck the doors."

"I can't understand what you're saying" I said, straining to make sense of his words.

"The doors. Are th-"

"What about the doors?" I hollered back.

The line went dead. I pulled the phone away from my ear and stared at it for a moment before placing it back on its cradle. Then, trying to shake off the weird feeling in my stomach, I began to straighten up the desk, stacking various piles of papers. A few moments later, I glanced around the office and, satisfied, began shrugging into my coat when the phone rang again. "Hello?" I answered quickly.

"Marian, are you alone?" the words rushed out of Barry like a tidal wave.

"I think so," I replied slowly. "Rory might-"

"Lock your doors until I get there," he interrupted me. "Now."

"What are you-"

"Damn it, Marian, just lock your doors until I knock," he barked. "Let me know when you're back. I'll wait."

Shaking, I put down the phone and began to pat my coat pockets, trying to figure out what I'd done with the keys. Finally locating them in my purse, I walked quickly down the stairs. Padding quietly across the studio, I scanned my key ring, looking for the one that could lock the main entrance, when suddenly there was a loud thud outside. I paused only for a second, running the last few steps to the door just as someone began to push it open from the other side.

I couldn't believe it. Alec had been murdered after all and now, the killer was coming back to finish the job.

Adrenaline began to course through my veins and with a loud cry, I threw myself at the door and pushed with everything that I had.

"Ow!" someone grunted from the other side. "What the-" I recognized the voice immediately.

"Rory!" I cried, flinging the door open and throwing my arms around his neck. This issued another grunt and he shifted the small box in his arms so he could balance it on his hip.

"Hey kid," he replied, patting my back with his now free hand. Kicking the door closed behind us, his eyes grew dark with concern. "What's going on?"

Sniffling, my hands shaking with fear, I tried to lock the door several times but couldn't fit the key into the lock.

Gently, Rory steadied my hand in his, flicked my wrist and withdrew the key. Without realizing it, I'd begun to cry, fat hot tears rolling down my face, but I couldn't form a sound.

Rory dropped the box and pulled me into his chest. "I was just 'round the corner," he told me. "I was picking up some of our old editions from storage. I was thinking a throwback theme for our anniversary issue next year and I wanted to get a head start on-"

Finally finding my voice, I let out a loud wail, which melted into considerable sobbing.

Rory pulled back and took me by the shoulders. "What's wrong?" he demanded with a small shake. "Are you hurt? Where's Addison? Did something happen?"

I shook my head and pointed up to the office, where Barry was still waiting for me to tell him I was safe. Goodness knows what he was thinking if he was able to hear any of this exchange. Rory followed me up the stairs and watched me pick the phone up off the desk, my sobs reduced to loud hiccups and the occasional sniffle.

"Marian?" I heard Barry ask. "Marian, are you okay?" I sniffled and nodded that I was, when Rory came and took the phone from my hand.

"Hello?" He asked. "Who is this?" A pause. "Oh, hey-a. Yup, yup she's okay, just seems pretty rattled. Mmmhmm. Mmhmm. Ah, okay. Sure, I'll take care of it. Thanks for the call. Bye."

I was mystified. "That's it?" I squeaked.

"Sounds like a girl at an office down the street was followed to her car and assaulted," he told me. "Barry was worried about you being here alone. He's sorry for scaring you."

I felt like I'd had the wind knocked out of me and was suddenly very, very tired. "I want to go home," I told Rory, grabbing for my purse. "Can you walk me to my car?"

"Of course," he said, holding out an elbow for me to grasp. I leaned on him gratefully and we made our way back down the stairs.

Once we were outside, I turned my face up to look at his. "I thought there'd been a mistake," I admitted. "I thought he was calling to say that someone had killed Alec."

"Thought you were next, did you?" he asked me with a gentle shove.

"Yeah," I laughed, sniffling. Then I shook my head and, without meaning to, started to cry all over again.

"Hey," Rory said, stopping in front of me and pulling me in for another hug. "Nothing is going to happen to you while I'm around." I heard the smile in his voice and was instantly grateful to have such a good friend. I nodded into his chest. We stood like that for a few minutes and when I pulled away, he offered me his elbow again and we continued to walk in silence down the lit street. When we reached my car, Rory opened the door for me.

Ducking inside and tossing my purse onto the passenger seat, I inserted my key into the ignition. Turning back to him, I smiled. "Thank you," I told him sincerely. "For

69

everything."

He shrugged and grinned sheepishly.

Returning the grin, I reached out to close the door, but he grabbed the frame with his hand. "Hey?" he asked me. "Do you ever think about just getting a gun?"

"What?" I asked incredulous. "No!" The thought was horrifying. While my father had given my brother and I the basic rundown of gun safety, I'd never felt comfortable with the power and liked to keep my distance. Besides, I knew plenty of cops, detectives and concerned citizens who carried guns on their person 24/7. Chances were that if I was in a bad situation, I'd have some firepower around me. With the exception of tonight, it seemed. Okay, perhaps Rory had a point.

He shrugged again. "Well," he told me, "if you ever find yourself in need, there's a gun under the files of my bottom drawer."

"You have a gun?" I asked. "In my studio?"

"Technically, it's in my cubicle," he responded "but yes, I have a gun." He gave me a knowing look. "We work in a rough neighborhood, kid. And you, of all people, should know that."

It was true. I'd taken my fair share of crime scene photographs in the area where our office was located. They tended to be further north, for the most part, but one could never be too sure.

With a grim smile, I closed my door and waved to Rory as I drove away.

Later that night, I sat on my couch eating a Snickers bar while I stared at Fred swimming back and forth. "You have it so easy," I told him through munches. "I don't see anyone encouraging you to buy a gun."

As far as I knew, my father had never had to fire his gun anywhere other than the shooting range. While he'd ensured that I was knowledgeable enough to be lethal, I just never had it in me as an adult to make the actual purchase. Still, I found myself turning Rory's words over in my head. It wouldn't be the first time he'd been right about something. Perhaps there was something to his summation of where our studio was located.

No. Shaking my head to clear the thoughts, I stuffed the remainder of the Snickers bar into my mouth and turned back to Fred. "I'm not going to let it get to me," I said between chews. "Alec wasn't even murdered. I'm being ridiculous."

My cell began to ring and vibrate wildly on the coffee table. "Hello?"

"How you holding up?" asked Barry.

I sighed. "I'm fine," chew, chew, "just jumpy, I guess."

There was a sigh on the other end of the line, then, "You didn't hear this from me."

71

I clutched the phone tighter and sucked in a breath, swallowing the rest of my candy bar. "If this is another one of your inane-"

"Marian, I just need you to be a little careful the next few days," Barry cut in.

"Careful?" I asked. "What do you mean careful? I'm always careful."

"I mean something isn't totally right with the body, Marian," he told me. "You need to be careful. You know. Be aware of your surroundings and all that."

My mind started to race and I felt the Snickers bar rolling around in my stomach. "What's wrong with the bo- with Alec?" I asked.

Barry lowered his voice. "The autopsy wasn't totally clean."

My heart began to pound. "But you said-"

"I know what I said, Marian," he hurried on. "That's the report I was given." I heard him sigh. "Unfortunately the new Captain heard that your dad was sniffing around. I was just trying to help. Anyway, the Captain- he's worried you're trouble and he knows that you and I talk."

"Trouble!" I huffed.

Barry sighed heavily. "Look," he said, his voice suddenly sounding old and tired. "I told you what I was told. I'm only calling you now because someone I trust told me different. You know as well as I do that nobody over here wants to be told how to do their job, especially the new Captain. Especially by a small-town guy like your dad.

That's not me being mean, that's just how it is. Don't tell anyone about this. Don't look into this. Tell your dad to quit sniffing around." He took a shaky breath. "Just be careful." He paused. "Lock your doors and all that."

My brain tinged. "Is this why you called me earlier?"

"Yes," he admitted. "Now listen to me. I know you didn't do this. But I know Rory and Addison about as well as I know the Queen of England."

"They're good people," I assured him. After a moment I paused, then continued with, "Rory told me he has a gun at the office."

"What?" Barry shouted into the phone. Then, "What?" he hissed more quietly.

"Yeah," I told him. "After you told him there was an assault down the street, he walked me to my car, asked if I had a gun, then when I said no, he told me that his was hidden in his file cabinet if I ever needed it." The silence was deafening. "He's not your guy," I insisted. "He may as well be my big brother." Barry didn't respond, so I hurried on. "And I've known Addison since we were in diapers. She's crazy, but not like this. She thinks too much. There's no way she could have been behind this, she'd never have been able to unwind enough to pull it off."

"What about the other girl?" he asked.

"Betsy?" I shook my head into the phone. "I don't know her all that well, but she's not exactly what I'd chalk up to be a cold blooded killer." We were both quiet for a few moments. "I guess it could be someone that neither of us suspects. Like the intern."

After a few more seconds of pondering, Barry heaved another sigh. "Look, Marian," he said quietly, "I trust you. That's why I'm telling you this. I trust that you know your coworkers, too. But questions are headed your way, and a lot of them, I imagine. Keep your mouth shut. Don't ask questions. Don't answer them."

"Are we suspects?" I asked, taken aback.

"Yes," he answered matter-of-factly. "Why do you think I'm asking you to lay low until all of this gets figured out?"

"But we didn't-"

"I believe you," he cut me off. "I don't know how or why they're linking it back to you just yet, but I can tell you that until this is all cleared up, you need to be careful." There was a pause. "You need to get a gun."

"Why does everyone keep saying that?" I seethed. "I'm not going to get a gun."

"Just think about getting one, will you?" he begged. "If it isn't any of you, I have no idea who it could be. Things are going to stay tight-lipped around here until your dad backs off, they find new evidence, one of you four winds up dead, or all of the above."

I gulped. He wasn't joking. "How long until toxicology is back?" I asked.

"It could still be a few weeks," he admitted. "Although, if they're thinking it could be someone on the inside, they're going to work a whole lot faster."

"I'm not even a salaried employee," I muttered. "Why is it

that I have to deal with this?"

"Don't plan on any work for a while," he said. "And think about getting that gun." He paused. "Oh, and Marian?"

"What?"

"You can't tell a soul about this conversation. Addison, Rory, your parents- keep your mouth shut, or I could lose my job. Do you understand me?"

I nodded and though he couldn't hear me, the other end of the line clicked and I found myself staring at my cell, even as it blinked that the call was over. I couldn't believe that this was happening. What could the police possibly have as evidence that made them consider us criminals? "Whatever it is, it must be a doozy," I told Fred. Disinterested, he maintained a mellow paddle near the bottom of his tank.

Laying my head back on the couch, still clutching my phone, I closed my eyes and tried to piece together the puzzle.

The week passed by me in a blur. Knowing that I was useless at faking upbeat emotions when my insides felt like they were turning out, I avoided the studio at all costs. Rory would sniff out my secret in a second. That was if Addison Dawes, undercover reporter, didn't hound it out of me first. I responded to texts with cheery punctuation and a lot of emoticons, hoping to cover the worry and fear I felt — I was drenched in it. I'd even gotten my gun permit and purchased a .45 Magnum, much to my mother's dismay. Meanwhile, my father had muttered something to me about being able to keep the porn nuts at bay and I took it as a token of approval.

With my bank account once again dropping below the level of comfort following my massive purchase, and no paid work from the police department in sight, I found myself home alone with a microwave lunch meal that Friday. I was due to the warehouse later that afternoon for our much belated but highly anticipated *Yummy Tummy* photo shoot. The fact that it would be with our gorgeous new model, Mika, nearly had me in conniption fits. I'd run through my outfit for the 100th time that morning, resisting the urge to spend my last dollars on an outrageous new dress and celebratory lunch to cheers our amazing find.

Still cloaked in my robe and slippers from the morning, I was leaning against the kitchen counter, slurping up a spaghetti noodle when there was a loud knock on my door. Setting the black tray down, I cinched my robe, fluffed my bed head and walked slowly over to the peephole just in time to witness another sharp rapping from the other side. "Marian!" Addison shouted from the other side. "I know you're in there. Open the door."

I swung it wide open. "What are you doing here?" I asked.

"I should ask you the same question," she replied. "Rory said you haven't been to the office at all since Tuesday."

I shrugged. "Oh just, super busy." She lifted an eyebrow and scanned over my attire. I clutched the front of my robe as my cheeks began to pink in embarrassment. "Well I have been. Busy. Not really today so much but this week. But this afternoon, I'm going in for the *Yummy Tummy* photo shoot. With Mika. And-"

"I know what's going on, Marian," she told me, holding up a hand to cut me off.

I felt my eyes widen. "Know- know what?" I asked, clearing my throat and trying to act nonchalant.

She rolled her eyes. "Please. The last time your texts were punctuated was 2004." Rats, she had me there. "You're really terrible at pretending everything is okay," she continued. "Even Rory knew something was up. Smiley faces in your texts to him? Are you 14?"

"Look, I'm not allowed to say-"

"It's poison," she said, cutting me off.

I was stunned into silence. Blinking in rapid confusion for a few moments, I processed her words. "Alec?" I asked. "How did you-?"

"I could really tell that something was off when you didn't want to get Mexican food on Wednesday night. You never turn down Pedro's." I shrugged. She had me there. "I asked Rory to call and let me know if you weren't in by noon yesterday. You're never not in the office, you know? I'm not stupid. When he let me know you'd been a no-show since he walked you to your car, he confessed that you'd been pretty upset at that time."

"I was not upset," I told her, crossing my arms.

"Rory and I compared notes yesterday over lunch." She went on, ignoring me. "The overly optimistic texts. The fact that you wouldn't call either of us back. You were obviously hiding something." A pause as she eyed me with a look that said you should know better by now. "Then Rory mentioned that Barry had been really cagey on the phone. That maybe Barry just wasn't telling Rory what he'd originally called to tell you."

I was staring hard at my slippers, willing my face to stop burning. The last thing I wanted was for Barry to get fired due to the fact that I was terrible at keeping my emotions in check.

"Barry won't get fired," she assured me, reading my mind. "I'm keeping it quiet until I have all of my facts straight."

"You probably know more than me at this point," I said.

"We'll see," she answered. From there, she told me that she'd called in a long overdue favor with an old friend who was now a major player for the Chicago PD. Through him, she'd managed to gather parts and pieces that Barry apparently wasn't privy to just yet. As it turned out, our dear friend Alec had made himself useful by sampling some of the delectable treats from *Yummy Tummy*, the bakery that had provided cupcakes for our exclusive spread. Unfortunately for him, the cupcakes had been poisoned.

"I didn't even know the models ate," I said in disbelief.

"Marian, focus," Addison said, snapping her fingers. "The bottom line is that our office is suspect."

I shook my head. "We shouldn't be!"

"I know!" she said, taking hold of my shoulders. "The question is, how do we prove anything different? Obviously, we're a tight knit group. They won't trust us individually and they won't trust us as a unit. If they're set on us, they could just build a case around it. We'd be finished."

This potential nightmare sank into both of us slowly and we just stared at each other until one of us was able to speak.

"They're looking at the wrong people!" I cried, frantic. "I know we didn't do this! Why haven't they looked into the bakery? Everything could have transpired there. If all the cupcakes were poisoned, maybe we were all supposed to die!"

"I'd thought of that," she said, looking out of my living room window. "That's why I made sure that getting word on any other potential leads was part of the favor."

I could tell that she had more but wasn't sure why she wouldn't spill the beans. It wasn't like Addison to make me pry for secrets, she usually spilled them out, excited that she knew things as a reporter that I didn't, even being so close to some individuals on the police force. "Well?" I asked her, crossing my arms. "Please, tell me that they are looking into other people."

She turned her eyes back to mine. "They're looking into other people," she responded slowly.

I felt the breath I didn't even realize I'd been holding release. "Anyone we know?"

"Oh, yeah," she answered, in a way that suggested I would shortly wish I'd never asked. "James Holden, owner of *Yummy Tummy Bakery*."

Silence swept the room. Suddenly, blood was pounding in my ears. I felt myself swaying ever so slightly before I reached out to grab the countertop with both hands. Leaning forward, I closed my eyes and tried to picture happy things. But picturing a beautiful hammock on a deserted Caribbean island was no match for the ugly words that had just flipped everything on its head. Something dawned on me and I jerked towards Addison. "Oh, my God!" I shouted at her, covering my mouth with my hand. "We have a date tonight. I'm going on a date with a

81

murderer!"

"That's not entirely true," she assured me.

"Who else could it be?" I almost burst into tears. I normally prided myself on being calm and collected but this was all getting to be too much.

She seemed to consider my question for a moment before saying, "I suppose our options aren't looking very good at the moment."

"Oh my God," I said again. "I have to cancel. I have to cancel my date right now!"

"Are you nuts?" she asked, squeezing my arm, staring at me aghast.

"Are YOU nuts?" I spat back, practically shoving away the contact. "I'm not going on a date with the guy who is trying to off us! He'll probably poison my sushi."

"Marian, you have to go," she told me, with complete sincerity. "We can't miss this opportunity."

"Opportunity?" I cried. "What are you talking about, opportunity? The only opportunity will be his opportunity to kill me!"

"You'll die knowing that Rory and I are safe," she responded. When I glowered back she threw her hands up in the air. "Oh for goodness sakes, I was kidding!" I perked up. "You'll be wired, we'll keep you safe." And just like that, I deflated again. "I'm going to have to call in another favor," she said, thinking out loud.

"I hate to think of how you earn these favors," I muttered, radiating hatred for the whole plan with every inch of my being.

She tossed her hair and unbuttoned the top button of her already burgeoning pink silky blouse. "However I need to," she told me breathlessly, blinking prettily.

Scowling, I once again clutched my robe. "I hate you." With that, I stalked off down the hall, towards the bathroom.

"I'll call you with details." She paused. "Be sure to pick up your phone!"

"I'm in a shoot starting in an hour," I huffed over my shoulder. "You'll have to leave a message."

Her eyes lit up. "Oh, that's right," she cooed. "I darn near forgot about that. In fact, I seem to recall asking Betsy to plan it that way so that I could partake in the viewing party."

Even though she couldn't see me from inside the bathroom where I was currently stripping down, I shook my head. "No way," I called, tossing my pajama top into the hallway. "You have phone calls to make. A plan to put together. My life to save. And you only have-" I checked the clock on the bathroom wall, "about five hours to do it. All of it."

When I was met with silence, I triumphantly poked my head around the corner of the door and grinned. "I'm risking my life tonight," I told her, "the least you could do is make sure you're not distracted while putting that plan together."

Her face told me that she'd much rather be distracted

but, instead of commenting, she nodded and let herself out of the front door, locking me in when she went.

Satisfied, I reached around the shower curtain and adjusted the water faucets. Closing the bathroom door, I allowed the room to become completely enveloped in steam — mirrors and all — before I stepped into the warm, soothing water, trying to let all of my insecurities about the rest of the day wash down the drain.

I'd stayed in the shower a little longer than I should have and, as a result; I was running late to the photo shoot. Not at all the impression I wanted to make on our gorgeous new model. Cursing as my car got stuck behind yet another vehicle driving disturbingly under the speed limit, I checked the dashboard clock, which still hadn't started running backwards. That was unfortunate. Craning my neck, I tried to catch a glimpse over the top of the car in front of me. Then, checking both mirrors, I dodged quickly into the right lane and sped around my incredibly slow adversary, resisting the urge to glare at said person menacingly. We Midwesterners can be quite passive aggressive.

Crawling through a red light on my right hand turn, I zipped the last few blocks to the studio and squealed into the lot, gravel crunching loudly beneath my tires. Leaping from the car, I flew around to the back, pulled out three different camera bags, slammed the trunk and raced inside, my damp hair flapping wildly behind me.

Inside, the lights were on. I took a moment to compose myself behind the black curtain that still blocked the entrance from our call earlier that week. Taking a deep breath, I reached up to pinch my cheeks, hitched up the cameras and walked into the studio, my head high. The place was empty. Disappointed, I put down my gear and began to shed my coat, knitted cap and gloves. "This guy better not stand us up, too," I muttered as I made my way to the coat rack, combing fingers through my hat hair. Curiously, there was a man's light brown leather jacket already neatly dressing a hanger.

A noise from behind startled me and I dropped the hanger I'd been holding, before whipping around to face the stairs. "Apologies," Mika called, descending them in one of our signature royal purple *Food Porn* robes. "I was a little early but Rory was kind enough to let me into the dressing room for hair and makeup. Betsy helped." He smiled, making me slack jawed and weak in the knees. "I think I'm ready to go, if you are?"

He was even more gorgeous than I remembered. Blinking rapidly, I realized that my jaw was still slightly open, drool pooling in my mouth. Clamping it shut, I bent to pick up the hanger I dropped, strung up my coat and turned back to face him, a bright smile now lighting up my face. "Absolutely," I responded. "Do you know the background behind this shoot?" He shook his head no, so I went on to explain. "This is a client that paid to have an exclusive feature. In other words, their pastries are the only ones that will be appearing in our publication for next month. They tacked on a little extra for our very best model." I held up one of the cameras I'd pulled from a bag. "That little extra bought me a brand new Canon."

"I'm your very best model?" Mika asked, now standing only a few inches away.

Swallowing, I smiled and replied as calmly as possible, "I guess we'll find out." Ha! I wasn't going to be baited.

Rory walked in just then. "Need help getting set up?" he called, hands in his pockets as he casually strolled towards us.

"That would be awesome!" I told him. "Help me get a few backgrounds in order, will you?"

Together, we flipped through our collection and, selecting several, we pushed and pulled them into order so that they could be easily flipped through. Next, I went over and pulled out several small mats and rugs, which I dropped with a loud grunt near my camera bags. Choosing a soft gray square of carpet, I unrolled it on the floor where Mika would stand in front of our first screen, a soft lavender with wisps of gray. Satisfied, I flipped off the overhead lights and turned on my large flash heads, which were softened at the moment by an opaque umbrella. "Perfect," I said quietly to myself as I surveyed our work.

"All done here?" Rory asked, brushing his hands against his jeans. I nodded. "Let me know before you walk out," he said, turning to walk back to his cubicle. "I'll take you to your car."

"Ready to go?" Mika asked from behind me. Still lost in the space I was creating, I simply nodded my head. A few seconds later, he shyly shuffled past me and stood on the carpet square, still swathed in his purple robe, which played beautifully off of his skin tone. Catching myself staring at the small V that revealed just a touch of skin on his upper chest, I averted my eyes to the card table, discreetly set up in a back corner of the room. It was dressed in beautiful pastries — cupcakes, petit fours, fruit tarts, chocolate cakes.

My stomach made a low gurgling noise. "Later," I promised it quietly. Then, picking up a delicate tart dressed in berries and a sparkling glaze, I made my way over to Mika. "Robe," I told him pointedly, staring him dead in the eye. His smile was unassuming and yet, I still found myself nearly fainting. I maintained eye contact while he stripped down to his boxers and tossed his robe off to the side of the studio. I could feel the heat radiating off of his body, his eyes studying me curiously as we both debated our next move.

Reaching out, I handed him the tart, lowered my gaze to the floor and stepped out of the light. This was ridiculous. I was a professional. I'd worked with hundreds of models over the years — some were even famous in addition to sexy. Surely I could handle just another sexy, shirtless man gallivanting around my studio in nothing but his boxer briefs. "Focus," I muttered under my breath. Slowly picking up my new camera, I made sure it was ready before I flipped the lens towards my subject. "Show me what you've got, Mister," I challenged.

Within seconds, I had at least 20 amazing shots. For as timid as he seemed during our past interactions, Mika was pure electricity behind a camera. By that I mean, is it hot in here or is that just my model?

The afternoon flew by. Setting the final pastry back on the table, Mika reached for his bathrobe as I flipped through my most recent shots on the camera display. Okay, as I pretended to flip through the most recent shots on my display. It was a shame he cinched the robe so tightly — I could have done with one last view of his chest before he went upstairs to get dressed. This shoot had been the closest I'd come to getting laid in…in…um. Horrified, I tried to think of the last time I'd had sex. Was it three years? I shuddered at the thought.

Lost in my thoughts, I hadn't even noticed that Mika had picked up a cupcake nearly drowning in its frosting and was walking towards me. "Do you think we can eat these?" he asked with an apprehensive grin, the magnetism he'd hosted behind the lens replaced with boy-next-door charm.

I blinked. Surely I had misheard. He couldn't possibly be the type to eat processed sugar. I let my eyes slide from his jaw line to the svelte muscular physique that rippled beneath his robe, to his taunt, dark legs.

"I have a weakness for sweets," he continued, shrugging, snapping me back to the present. A curl fell softly against his forehead, which he gently blew back into place before breaking into a huge grin that nearly caused me to drop the camera. I could only nod my approval. The only ones that ever ate from the displays were Rory, Addison and myself. Okay, mainly me. I distractedly set a hand on my growling stomach, which protruded slightly from the confines of my trendy slacks, and looked forlornly at the elegant treats, then back to Mika as I briefly wondered how often he worked out to keep that body and still indulge in his weakness. I worked out purely for the benefit of being able to eat what I wanted, not to be toned.

Not even bothering to remove the wrapper, Mika raised the cupcake to his lips and went to lick at the frosting. I watched him, mesmerized by the complete and utter sensual ridiculousness of the entire situation. He caught me staring before I had the chance to look away and paused, his mouth poised to take a bite. Lowering the cupcake slowly from his lips, his eyes flashed with something that felt wild and sensual. "Would you like some?" he asked me. Without waiting for an answer, he dipped his finger into the creamy chocolate frosting and held his finger out to me.

Feeling very awkward and oddly aroused, I placed my camera on the display table and reached out to scrape his offering onto my own finger but he pulled away, shaking his head, just as I reached for his hand.

"Open your mouth," he whispered.

Was he serious? This was quite possibly every romance novel I'd ever read (okay, I don't read the whole book, just certain chapters, but this was how they all started, right?) come to life. It couldn't be real. Ouch! I thought, pinching my nails deep into my upper arm. It was slightly flabby. I really didn't need the added calories. Then again, what was a little lick? Five sit-ups? Six? Darting a furtive glance towards the upper office as well as the entrance to cube land, I swallowed and turned back to Mika. Surely I'd be breaking company policy if I licked frosting from the finger of a professional model. Then again, if such rules existed, I probably invented them back when Addison was being loved often and I was spending Fridays with a pint of mint chocolate chip watching *You've Got Mail* for the umpteenth time whilst crying to a very bored Fred. Ah, hell. I only live once. And apparently I hadn't lived at all in the last three years.

I opened my mouth at just about the same point as my earlier conversation with Addison dawned on me. Gasping, I slapped Mika's hand away. Surprised, he also dropped the cupcake. He stared at it for a moment, before looking back to me confused.

"Sorry!" I said horrified, kneeling to scrape up the cupcake. Could I contract poison through touch? Mika must think I'm a total nut job. I paused, unsure of what to do. When he knelt to help, I practically threw my body across the mess. "I just remembered!" I shouted at him, desperately searching for an explanation for my sudden loss of manners. How did you explain to someone that their predecessor had been murdered? You couldn't. Not without scaring them off. Call me selfish, but I wasn't ready for this one to disappear. "I promised to send all of this back to the bakery! Tomorrow! For their window display!" Was that plausible? Did *Yummy Tummy* even have a window display? Chances are that if I didn't know,

Mika wouldn't either. I hoped.

He seemed to accept my bizarre explanation, even as I tottered, trying not to fall into the mess. "In that case, how about dinner tonight?" he asked me. Casual. Collected. Like he hadn't just asked a crazy person on a date. "I know a place that serves the most amazing cheesecake. If we can't eat dessert here, it only makes sense to find some elsewhere."

Something inside of me stirred. "Dinner!" I cried, smacking my forehead with my palm. Turning, I grabbed for my purse, which was laying on the floor, and began to dig frantically through it for my cell. Six missed calls. One voicemail. All from Addison. Smiling apologetically, I opened my voicemail app and held the phone closely to my ear, not wanting him to overhear a single word of the conversation.

"Pick up your phone, you saucy minx!" Addison chirped the opening line of her message. "I'll be at the studio around 5:30 to give you the plan and get you wired. Be ready!"

Irritated, I closed out of the app and turned back to Mika. Just my luck that a beautiful model who actually ate would ask me out on the same night I had to go on a date with a murderer. "I can't," I said, tossing my phone back into my purse. "I already have plans."

"I'm not surprised," he replied, easily. I blushed and looked away. "How about tomorrow night?"

Ah, persistence. I was planning my outfit already.

Assuming I made it home alive. "Tomorrow is perfect," I told him.

"Great." That smile again. "Let me help you clean this up."

My eyes locked on his gorgeous, smooth hands, completely free of any blisters or burns. Who knew how he managed that, being around wood and power tools all day? "No!" I cried, fending him off from the mess again. "I mean, I can get this. Really just a one person job. No need to get dirty. I mean to dirty you up. I mean get your hands dirty."

He gave me that crooked smile and I was lost in a daydream. "Well, in that case, I'm going to go get dressed. I'll just meet you back here tomorrow. Maybe around six?"

"That's great."

"Great." There was a nervous pause and we both laughed. "Well…great," he said, turning and heading for the stairs. "I'll see you tomorrow at six."

I resisted the urge to wave goodbye but, once he'd shut the dressing room door, I let out a small squeal of glee and did a little dance around the studio.

"My, my, my, aren't we excited to be walking into the lion's den," Addison called to me from where she stood by the entrance.

I stopped quickly and whirled to face her. "You're early!" I said, surprised.

She checked her watch. "Actually, I'm right on time," she responded, striding towards me confidently. Then, with a knowing grin she asked, "Good shoot?"

"The best," I crowed. I checked to make sure the door to the dressing room was closed before I grabbed for her hands and started jumping up and down. "He asked me out!"

She grinned, knowingly. "I knew he'd go for you."

"I don't know what you're talking about," I muttered.

"Please! You've got brains, talent-"

"And the modeling industry truly believes in inner beauty. What with all the airbrushing and such," I tossed back, slapping her playfully on the behind as I moved to pack up my camera, which was still sitting among the sweets. Nodding to her tight, bright ensemble, I added, "You trying to earn a spot in next month's edition?"

"What are you suggesting? I've got brains and talent!" she fired back as she tugged at the hemline of her curve-hugging pencil skirt.

"You wouldn't know it under all that," I retorted playfully, pointing to her barely there — but somehow still professional — outfit.

"I have enough brains and talent to piece together a plan that will keep you from getting murdered in short order." She turned her gaze down to her perfect bubblegum pink manicure and began picking at the edges.

"You should probably fill me in on that," I agreed. Looking down at the mess that was still on the floor, I decided that a safer approach was better. If only I could find some paper towels.

Digging in her purse, Addison produced a small black box, which she handed to me. I opened it, revealing a beautiful pewter pin shaped like a looped ribbon. "It's your audio," she told me when I fingered it cautiously. Gently pulling it out of the box, she pressed the back of it before pinning it to my shirt. "You're live," she told me. "Richard and I will be able to keep tabs on you as long as you stay within about two miles."

"Richard?" I asked.

"My version of Barry, but he's with the Chicago PD. Works Narcs. He came up to help me out with this special favor for a little stray from the usual cases of drugged-up hookers and crazed drug lords."

"Nothing too special, I hope," Rory called to us, strolling around the corner from his cubicle. Betsy lagged behind him, an angry scowl on her face as she clutched her clipboard, which she seemed to be permanently attached to these days.

Addison smiled at him. "Probably not special in the same way you'd prefer."

He blushed and ducked his head quickly. Since when was she making sexual quips towards Rory?

Betsy made a low, disgusted noise in the back of her throat and Addison quickly turned her attention towards our disgruntled intern. "Haven't seen you around much this week," she said, a little too sweetly. "What have you been up to?"

"Home," Betsy snapped back. "Where I was told to stay

for a few days."

"So kind of you to make it into the internship that counts towards your college credits," Addison responded, shrugging off Betsy's attitude. "Which reminds me, you have a journal coming up due to your advisor, correct? I suggest you find enough work to fill your pages so that I have something to sign off on — now that you're not modeling and all."

Huffing, Betsy turned and stalked back towards the cubicles. Once she was out of earshot, Rory turned to us. "I don't know what has gotten into her," he said, shaking his head. "Surely she can't still be upset over the other day."

"There wouldn't even be an issue if someone had created the call correctly," I told him pointedly.

"She still would have tried," Addison muttered.

"How much longer is her term with us?" I sighed.

Addison shrugged and sighed. "I can never remember when school ends. November, December." She frowned. "Or is their break now in January?" She flipped her hand as if to say who knows? "But really, what kind of administrative help can you expect to get for free? We'll have to check out her application again next week. But tonight…we have things to do."

I broke from the group to grab a roll of paper towels and quickly picked up the cupcake blob that was slowly melting onto the floor.

"What happened here?" Rory asked.

"Don't want to talk about it," I muttered, tossing the whole mess into a trashcan. "So, for tonight, what-"

We all turned when we heard footsteps on the upper landing. As Mika descended the stairs, the three of us watched him, not wanting to continue any of our conversations among outside ears. Besides, he was just so incredibly lovely to watch. Smooth. Graceful. Gorgeous. Approaching us, he smiled. "I just wanted to say thanks again," he said kindly to all of us. Stepping around our little circle, he retrieved his jacket, which hung just next to mine. It was fate! As he pulled it on, he directed his smile to me. "And I'm really looking forward to tomorrow."

I smiled back and felt the blush rising in my cheeks. "Me too," I told him sincerely.

"What's tomorrow?" asked a deep voice. Stepping around the black curtain and into the studio was James.

Panicked, I turned to Addison, my eyes practically bugging out of my head. "What are you doing here? I thought we were meeting at the restaurant." My eyes still focused on Addison, I added, "You're really early."

"Turn around," she mouthed as discreetly as possible. We had a brief stare down before I turned my smile up to full wattage and spun to face him. Rory, who was beginning to understand, crossed his arms amusedly and waited.

James and Mika were focused intently on each other. No one moved. Just as I thought the room would explode with testosterone, James turned to me. "I wanted to surprise you," he said. "I thought we could walk over to the

97

restaurant together. It's only a few blocks."

A vein in Mika's neck bulged slightly and he narrowed his eyes, shifting his gaze from James to me and back to James. I swallowed hard as Addison started to fan herself and took a seat on a nearby stool. It was pretty hot. I'd never had two men into me at the same time, let alone two mind-numbingly gorgeous men. Still, one of them was probably an axe murderer, which kind of put a damper on the situation. "Mika, this is James," I stammered, as my legs locked in fear. Maybe I shouldn't be introducing the two. "James owns *Yummy Tummy*, the place we have the exclusive with for next month."

Mika's face relaxed slightly and he held out his hand to shake James's. "Oh, you bake," he said in a way that suggested he wasn't overly impressed.

James gave him a tight smile and took his hand with slightly more force than was necessary. "Actually, I just own it." He paused and cut his eyes to me quickly before looking back to James. "I own a lot of things in this town. Where did you say you were from?"

Mika pulled his hand away. "I didn't," he responded.

"James, this is Mika," I said helpfully, breaking the tension. "Mika is our-"

"Model," Mika finished. "You did ask for the best."

"The manager probably requested that," James replied smoothly. "He takes care of all of the advertising."

I turned to Addison, my eyes wild with fear. I hadn't even heard the full plan. Should I walk with him? That would mean I'd probably be walking back with him following dinner. In the black of night. What was I supposed to talk to him about? Should I just be casual? Was I supposed to try to draw out a confession? How was I supposed to remain focused, anyway?

Addison grabbed my arm and smiled brightly. "Well, gentlemen. I'll let you two chat. I need to borrow Marian for just a second." With that, she was tugging me urgently across the studio, Rory following in hot pursuit. We rounded the corner and she drug me past the cubicles, into the development room. Once Rory was inside, she shut the door with a soft thud. "Was it just me or was that really hot?" she asked, eyes glazing over.

I snapped my fingers in front of her face. "Focus!" I cried. "What's the plan?"

"Wait, you're not going to walk with him are you?" Rory asked, his face frowning with worry.

"No!" I shouted at the same time Addison shouted, "Of course!"

"What?!" we said, looking at each other.

Addison put a hand on my shoulder. "This is perfect," she told me.

"It's getting dark!" I bleated. "This is not perfect. This is a time to panic. I'm panicking."

Addison motioned to my pin. "We will know exactly where you are the whole time," she said.

"Not if he drags me outside your paltry two-mile radius," I snapped.

"She's right, Addison," Rory started. "She's not-"

"Oh, who asked you?" Addison growled, fixing him with a dark look. Turning back to me and taking me by the shoulders, she said, "Look, we're not even sure he did it. I put myself in dangerous situations like this all the time to get stories."

"Who else could have-" I began, but she held up a finger to silence me.

Gently stroking my hair, she looked me straight in the eye. "That's what we have to find out," she told me. "Right now, you're our best shot."

I stared back at her before sighing in defeat. "That's your whole plan?" I asked. "I just have to go along with everything?"

She nodded. "I have Richard. He has access to backup if we need it. Other than you catching him trying to slip something into your food, or him dragging you into a back alley, we have no idea how else to catch him."

"So I'm bait?" I asked. When there was no response, I muttered, "Can you guys hear me on this?" as I tapped the pin.

"Crystal clear," she assured me, pressing a finger to her ear. The listening device must have already been set up and turned on.

"I can't believe this stupid plan took you nearly five hours to formulate," I fumed.

She seemed to hesitate as if she wanted to add something, but instead replied, "I'm going to head out the back door.

I'll be with you the whole time." With a wink she added, "Don't make me regret that decision."

"I can't tell if you're encouraging me to sleep with him or not." I reached around her for the door knob and added, "Your sex life must be really atrocious if your hopes are pinned to me."

Rory coughed as Addison eyed me with a sly smile as she practically waltzed out the door. "I've never had any such thing" she promised.

Shooing Rory out the door, I took a moment to collect myself, then strode confidently back into the studio, where both men still stood, arms crossed, frowning at one another. When they heard me approaching, they immediately dropped their arms and turned to face me with equally endearing smiles.

"Are you ready?" James asked, holding out his elbow.

Mika turned and snatched my coat from its hanger, holding it open for me. As he helped me slip it on, he gave me a gentle squeeze on my shoulder, whispering, "I'll see you back here tomorrow night." With a nod to James, he slipped around the curtain and out the front doors.

Still holding out his elbow, James smiled. "I was starting to worry he'd tag along," he told me. With a wolfish grin, he eyed my blouse upon which I'd undone an extra button prior to the photo shoot. Embarrassed, I tugged at the shirt with my free hand, trying in vain to piece it back together with one hand. Unlooping our arms, he moved in front of me and buttoned me back up. I smiled shyly and cinched my coat closed before taking his arm and walking with him towards the door. Something about him felt incredibly dangerous and yet, I couldn't help but wonder if I'd made it all up in my head. Maybe he wasn't even our guy.

Out front, a shiny black pickup truck sat waiting for us by the curb. Guiding me towards it, he opened the door and smiled. "Get in."

I swallowed hard and tried to steady my voice. "I thought we were walking." With a laugh, I nervously added, "It's only a few blocks."

"I actually have a different place in mind," he offered by way of explanation. "Come on, hop in." A pause before he broke into a gorgeous smile that reached all the way up to those emerald eyes. "I won't bite."

"It's just- I mean- I was really looking forward to sushi," I told him pathetically as my mind raced. What was I supposed to do? Addison didn't cover this!

"Me too. But I thought about it and think we should start fresh." With a laugh, he came over and put his hand in the small of my back, guiding me to his truck. "Come on."

Hoisting myself into the cabin, which smelled overpoweringly like vanilla, I silently hoped that Addison was, in fact, privy to the entire conversation and that she and Richard were set to roll. "Where are we going?" I asked.

"It's a surprise," he answered, closing the door behind me. I suddenly hated surprises.

As he walked around the back of the truck, searching for

his ignition key, I whispered menacingly into the pin. "I hope you know that if I make it out of this alive, I'm going to kill you. And your little dog, too. That means you, Richard."

As we sped through the streets, I did my best to nonchalantly mention the intersections we paused at, hoping that Addison and Richard could still hear me. James seemed amused by my nervous commentary, which I took as a bad sign. He knew exactly what I was up to. He was totally going to kill me.

Instead of driving us to some creepy place in the middle of nowhere, however, he pulled his Ram into a parking lot overflowing with cars of every color, shape and size.

"Where are we?" I asked, trying to find a sign or banner on the shoddy wooden structure that looked ready to sink in on itself at any moment.

James just smiled and came around to open my door. Holding out a hand to help me out of the truck, he said, "We are at the best little seafood joint in the city. Amazing fish and chips." With a smile, he added, "You never struck me as the frilly type."

For a moment, I was wrought with memories of our escapades just out of college and I wondered if he was thinking the same thing. Subconsciously, I rubbed softly at my lower back despite the fact that it hadn't been repeatedly hitting a seatbelt buckle in ages.

James wrapped an arm around my shoulders casually

105

and we walked towards the entrance where a small group of teenagers huddled with laughter and loudness. The girls broke their gazes towards my date as we walked by and one of them scowled at me, eyeing my gray pants, which suddenly felt incredibly dowdy. James had shown up so suddenly, I hadn't even had time to powder my nose. Nervously, I reached for the door, but James blocked my hand.

"Let me," he said, opening it with a gallant gesture that the establishment probably hadn't seen in, well, ever.

Inside, the restaurant looked about how one would expect. Tables were shoved together haphazardly, the paint peeled from the walls, and old frazzled waitresses were running from table to table as boisterous drunks shouted their orders and clutched tightly to their beer mugs. Not quite as romantic as *Kabuki*, but then, what did I expect? I'd already slept with the man, it wasn't like he needed to impress me. Plus he was probably a pathological killer, a hobby that surely didn't pay much.

James and I found an abandoned two top near the back of the establishment. He helped me out of my coat before hanging it and his own on a discreet hook on the wall. Once he'd ensured that my chair was properly pushed in, he went and sat on the other side of the table. His mannerisms seemed far too developed for a murderer. Still, I'd need to stay on my guard. The charm could just be part of his ploy to wear down my defenses. Who knew what he'd attempt to do to me later? My mind briefly turned to a naughty fantasy before I shook myself out of it and locked eyes with James, who sat with a bemused smile on his face.

"Where were you just now?" he asked, curiously.

"Nowhere. Nothing," I stammered, picking up a menu which had been left by a waitress old enough to be my grandmother. It was yellowed with age and splattered with a variety of stains that I could only hope were caused by ketchup. The inside was packed with baskets, platters and plates of every kind of fish — available steamed, grilled, fried or blackened. The variety of southern-style sides ranged from mac and cheese to fried okra to fresh cut rosemary fries. The place may look like a dump, but they sure had their menu down. Hopefully it would all taste just as good as it sounded.

Once our orders were placed, we had nothing to do but wait and talk. We chatted for a few minutes about families and mutual acquaintances from our college days. My complete inability to hide my emotions made me nervous and I was worried he'd read my mind, rampant with accusations, at any moment. "What were you doing at my apartment?" I found myself blurting out once the small talk had run dry. Ah, subtlety.

He looked surprised by my outburst, but quickly flattened it away and smiled. "I had no idea that, that was your apartment," he responded smoothly. Something in his reaction told me he was lying.

Nonetheless, he brushed off my curious look and crossed his arms, defiant. His purple button-down pulled tight across his chest and his upper arms bulged slightly. I swallowed. This wasn't going to be any easier than our last date. It didn't matter that he'd possibly chop me up later and store me in his freezer for stew, his magnetism was grossly alluring and on full volume. It wasn't fair to his victims. It really wasn't.

"I'd been visiting someone," he continued, his green eyes darkening.

I made a noise somewhere in the back of my throat. "Another woman?" I asked. He smiled and shrugged. The nerve. "Nothing too serious, it seems," I replied. He shrugged again. Narrowing my eyes, I felt my temper flaring but tried to keep it under control, using my newfound disgust to fuel the conversation into something that Addison could use. "Well," I said as controlled as possible, "what's new with you?"

He seemed disoriented by the change in subject and I took momentary satisfaction in his confusion. "Working a lot," he said, reaching for his water, which our waitress had left in addition to our beers.

I nodded in encouragement. "You own a bakery now," I said, feigning excitement. "How did you get into that?"

"Business ownership?" he asked, taking another swig of his water. "Just stumbled into it. My partner decided to take his early fortune and retire. I took mine and turned it into more opportunities."

My forehead wrinkled in confusion. "I had no idea that the baking business was so lucrative," I told him sincerely.

He chuckled. "I'm involved in far deeper investments."

Something about what he'd just said clicked. "What do you mean?" I asked, hoping that Addison and Richard were recording every single word.

James fixed me with a look that was tuned somewhere between a poker face and smoldering desire. I swallowed hard and my hand slowly drew to the top button of my blouse, which had somehow become undone again, showing off my slightly flushed chest. I clutched it closed tightly, which broke the spell. "Nothing to worry about," he murmured as he glanced around the room. "Will you excuse me for a moment?" He stood and strode confidently towards the restrooms.

"Was that code?" I hissed, lowering my mouth to the pewter ribbon still pinned to my shirt. Did he know that I was onto him? Had he meant that I shouldn't be worried about getting killed later or I shouldn't worry about what line of business he was in outside of baking cookies because I'd find out soon enough? Panic was welling up in my chest and I felt crazed, taking in all the possible exits of the restaurant. If you counted the small, slightly cracked window behind the bar, there were two. This place really wasn't up to fire code. Still, it's not like I could get anywhere. Who knew how far away Addison and Richard were?

Our waitress came and plopped two plates of steaming hot seafood on the table, along with a bottle of ketchup she had tucked into her apron. Everything looked and smelled incredible. My stomach growled, reminding me that the last meal I'd had was a paltry Lean Cuisine for lunch. It seemed like just that afternoon had been so very long ago.

James reappeared suddenly and rubbed his hands together as his eyes grazed over his huge plate of crab legs. Smiling, his gaze met mine. "Looks delicious," he said, his voice low. I gulped. He wasn't talking about his dinner.

Somehow I managed to clear away the cobwebs of fear that were slowly being sewn throughout my brain and carried on a normal, if slightly dry, conversation through dinner. Perhaps if I bored him to death, he'd lose interest. Unfortunately, it just seemed to make him more curious, as if I were intentionally shrouding myself with mystery.

Once we'd eaten our fill and our water glasses sat empty, the ice slowly melting and molding together like a game of Tetris, I excused myself and made my way to the bathroom. Checking under the stalls to make sure no one was within earshot; I pulled out my phone and called Addison. "Get back out there," she scolded me in welcome.

"Where are you?" I wailed. "I didn't even know if you guys were behind us."

"Of course we were behind you," she snapped. "You only slipped your location into the conversation with James about every third block."

"Do you think he noticed?" I asked.

Addison sighed in frustration, but sucked in a deep breath. Suddenly there was a slight scuffle on the other end of the line, before I heard a different voice. "Just try to

110

relax," said a gravely older male, who I could only assume was Richard. "I've been at this a long time. If I thought you were in danger, I'd get you out. He's not going to kill you in the middle of the most popular hole-in-the-wall Milwaukee has."

There was another scuffle and Addison's voice came back on the line. "Things are being handled," she assured me. "I just need you to get out there and keep him occupied. Okay?"

I nodded and sighed. "Okay," I breathed, clicking off. Tucking my phone back into my pocketbook, I took a moment to glance in the mirror. Smoothing a few loose strands of hair back behind my ears, I squared my shoulders and looked directly at my reflection. "Let's get this over with."

Stepping out, I paused at the corner and peeked around to the dining room, my eyes stopping on our table. James had been accosted by the young girl who'd given me a dirty look on our way in. She was incredibly beautiful but James didn't seem the least bit interested, completely ignoring her flirtatious advances. Ha, I thought, quietly walking towards our table. The moment he caught me striding towards him, he suddenly lit up with interest towards our new young friend and even seemed to begin flirting back. "You've got to be kidding me," I muttered.

As I approached, he mocked surprise and embarrassment over my arrival. Before the girl left, she wrote her number on a cocktail napkin and tucked it deep into his shirt pocket with a grin, then fixed me with another dirty look as she slithered back to her table. I wanted to punch her.

"Some things never change," he told me patting his pocket with a mischievous sparkle to his eye. "Are we ready to go?" He pushed himself up and came around the table to grab our coats. I snatched mine away and pulled it on myself before steaming my way out the front door. He clearly had no interest in the girl, despite his comment, so why pretend? Was he hoping that reminding me that he was a playboy would win him favor later tonight? If so, he had another thing coming. I wouldn't be played and murdered. Oh, no. One thing at a time.

I was so red with rage that I didn't speak at all on our drive back to town. Thankfully, I noticed that he was keeping to main roads. "No dictation this time?" he asked playfully. I turned to glower at him and noticed the tinge of worry that crinkled the corner of his eyes. Let him worry, I thought huffily, turning to look back out the passenger side window and into the dusky blanket of evening.

We arrived back at the warehouse without incident and I immediately reached for the door handle once we'd come to a stop by the entrance. "Wait," James said, leaning across the cab to close it. I took a deep breath and forced myself to turn silently to him, waiting for him to finish. "I just- I didn't mean to-" his eyes were filled with remorse. "Marian, I'm sorry," he said simply. "That was completely uncalled for."

I found myself believing his apology immediately and

hated myself for it. "I need to go," I told him, pulling the handle and stepping out of the truck. "Thanks for dinner and for beer and for driving." I shut the door hard and lowered my head to the wind as I made my way down to the parking lot.

I heard his engine whirring behind me as he crept along, following me to my car. Surely I couldn't have made it all the way out of his truck only to have him do away with me now. I picked up my pace slightly, but his truck didn't lose ground. Eventually, my steps turned into a brisk jog and I clutched at my pocketbook as I hurled myself down the sidewalk.

"Marian," James called out the passenger window, which was now completely rolled down. "What are you doing?"

I paused at the edge of the sidewalk, panting, and glanced to my right. My car was parked at the far end of the lot, close to the alley and second entrance to our building. Knowing that I could make it, even if it meant I'd have to run, I spun around and faced James, my face tight with anger. "Leave me alone," I told him with all of the force I could muster. The wind nipped hard at my thin pants and I hugged my body, trying to keep all the warmth from escaping.

"Marian, get back in the truck and let's talk about this," he pled.

I scoffed and began to dig around for my keys. "I'm not getting in there," I told him, pawing through the contents of my purse. "I saw you start talking to that girl the second

I walked around the corner. What suddenly brought the interest? Hmm?"

He seemed to redden slightly in the darkness. "I didn't know you saw all of that."

"What kind of excuse is that?"

"I'm sorry!"

I laughed bitterly. "I'm not interested in anything that you have to say to me. Not anymore." Finally digging my keys out of a side pocket, I looked up into James's perfect green eyes and went to hit my remote start button, hoping to shake the chill in the air before I climbed in. "I'll talk to you-"

Suddenly, there was a loud explosion from the parking lot. My eyes locked with James's and I saw an orange fireball reflected back at me, his mouth forming an "O" of surprise before the sheer draft of heat knocked me to the ground. Everything went white.

I awoke slowly, the harsh fluorescent lights above me only serving to increase the throbbing pain on the left side of my forehead. Blinking, I raised a hand and attempted to shield my eyes.

"She's awake," a voice called loudly. I winced in pain. "Sorry," the voice said to me, placing a cold compress to my head.

"Where am I?" I asked, trying hard to orient myself.

"An ambulance," the voice replied. "Outside of your office." My eyes adjusted and I recognized the dark-skinned female EMT who was busy wrapping my arm in a blood pressure cuff. "Do you remember anything that happened?"

I shook my head and the effort caused me to grimace. What the heck was going on? My arm felt sore with pressure as she pumped the cuff with air and held a stethoscope to the crook of my arm, listening for my pulse.

The last thing I could remember, I'd been walking back to my car. James had dropped me off. There had been an argument about something. "Oh my God," I moaned, the whole evening flooding my brain at once. "Did my car explode?"

"Marian." I recognized Addison's voice, filled with

concern.

I tried to push myself up off the stretcher bed, but groaned and flopped backwards. Gingerly, I touched my forehead, where I could feel a hot sticky mess near my temple. "Don't touch that," the EMT chided me gently. "I'm trying to clean you up."

"Will she need stitches?" Addison asked anxiously, climbing into the ambulance beside me.

"No, just looks like a nasty face plant," the EMT said, as she dabbed at my injury. With a grin she added, "Luckily she caught herself with her forehead, not her teeth." Addison and I just stared at her.

Eventually, I slowly rolled my head towards my friend. "Addison, what happened to my car?" I asked, wincing slightly at the pain my own voice caused my head. "And where's James?"

Her lower lip began to tremble as she took my hand. "He's being questioned," she told me. "Your car is…um, it's gone."

"I'd been hoping this was all just some kind of sick dream. Ow!" I cried, tensing as the EMT smeared a clear jelly across the gash on my forehead.

"Ow," Addison whimpered as I squeezed her hand just a little too tightly.

"Sorry," the EMT said to both of us. Then to me, "Just hold still."

Loosening my grip on Addison's hand, I waited for her to continue. "The police seem to think that someone slipped an explosive into your car. It was probably intended to go off when you slipped the key in the ignition, but something set it off early, thank goodness."

"My remote starter," I told her. "I went to start my car while James and I were arguing."

"Okay, you're all done," the EMT told me. As I went to sit up, however, she grabbed gently at my shoulders and held me down. "I really think you should go to the hospital and get checked out."

I waved her off and tried to sit up again, but Addison laid a hand on my chest. "Just think about it while you lay here for a few minutes, okay?" she pled.

I grumbled, but remained prone on the stretcher while the EMT went about cleaning up the cabin. Minutes later, I heard fast-paced footsteps and Rory's voice shouting, "Where is she? Where is she?"

"We're in this one," Addison called out to him.

"Addison," I groaned. "Stop yelling."

"Sorry," she whispered, giving my hand a quick kiss.

Suddenly Rory's head was bobbing at the entrance to the ambulance. "Oh, Marian. How are you? How is she?" he asked, darting glances between the preoccupied EMT and Addison.

"She'll make it," said the EMT. "But I really think she needs to go get everything checked out at the hospital." With that, she stepped out and made her way to another ambulance which was parked just across the way.

My friends looked at me expectantly. "I'd rather not," I

told them, huffily. "I'm perfectly fine."

"The department will cover it," said Barry with a grin, coming up behind Rory.

"Barry!" I whooped before closing my eyes with a whimper.

"Good to see you, Moyer," he told me, then nodded at Rory and Addison. "Folks," he said with another smile which seemed somewhat forced.

"They're not still thinking it's us, are they?" I asked him through waves of pain.

"Hard to say," he told me. "No one's going to tell me much of anything." He turned around to glance at his fellow officers as they milled around in our parking lot. Sighing, he turned back to me. "Look, the reality is that one of you could have crafted it all up." Addison cried out in strangled protest and her left eye twitched slightly. Barry held up a hand, waiting for her to finish before he continued. Rory climbed into the cabin behind her and rubbed Addison's upper back soothingly as she took a few deep breaths. Her angry grip on my hand loosened. Barry continued. "But I would like to think, considering how close Marian came to being a flaming dessert, that they are looking harder at other leads."

"What about James?" Addison asked, frantically.

"Addison!" I admonished. "What about him? We were together the whole night. He couldn't have."

She shook her head. "You were supposed to meet him at the restaurant," she reminded me. "Plus, he was early. And

how did he even know where we're located, anyway?"
Rory was nodding in agreement and Addison continued
on, encouraged. "He would have seen your car the other
morning when he asked you out. He'd know exactly what
you were driving."

It was all fitting into place after all. "He told me at dinner
that he was involved in deeper investments," I added.

"That he used to have a partner," Addison told Barry and
Rory excitedly.

"But that his partner had invested his part of their first
fortune in retirement," I continued. "And that he had
invested in more business. What if he's a hit man?"

Barry looked confused as he switched his gaze between
Addison and I. "Did you both go on a date with him?" he
asked, scratching his head.

Addison shrugged and smiled sheepishly. "Kind of," she
told him. Delicately, she reached over and removed my
pewter pin and placed it into Barry's hands. "I was kind of
recording it."

His eyes bugged out of his head and he darted a glance
behind him to ensure that no one had heard. "You can't do
that," he told us angrily, once he was satisfied that we had
no eavesdroppers. Turning back to Addison and I, he
pulled himself into the cabin. "What were you thinking?"

Addison snorted. "I was thinking that I'm an undercover
reporter. I was thinking that James is a suspect."

"How did you come to that conclusion?" Barry hissed but
Addison silenced him with a look.

119

"It's my job," she said simply. "Isn't it the least bit curious that he showed up just as everything started happening? Does he seem like the type to own a bakery of all things?" We all craned our necks around the ambulance doors to catch a peek at James, who had his arms crossed as he spoke with a senior looking detective. James caught us staring suspiciously and gave us a hesitant wave. With tight smiles, we waved back and slowly drew ourselves back into a huddle inside the ambulance.

Addison continued. "Our model was poisoned. Next thing you know, Marian found James sniffing around outside her apartment-"

"Not exactly," I told them.

She snorted. "He asks her on a date because he knows that'll distract her." I cried out in protest but she fixed me with a look. "I'm sorry, honey, but it's true." Turning back to Barry she continued. "He intends to meet her at the restaurant, but shows up to the warehouse? He's shady about his business ventures? He demonstrates manners all night until he drops her off, not at her car, where he'd be a sitting duck until she started it and left, but at the entrance to her office?"

"Maybe he thought she'd need to get something from inside," Barry protested.

Addison just shook her head. "You make up all the excuses you want to make for him," she responded. "But I'm still suspicious."

We all pondered in silence for a few moments and then I

slowly pushed myself up on the gurney with a moan.

"Lay down," Rory said gently.

I shook my head and the effort made me slightly dizzy, but I was determined to get out of there. "I'm not going to the hospital. And I can't stay in here. I will not just sit around waiting when someone out there is trying to kill me. He could poison my IV! Inject me with penicillin! I'm allergic, you know. He probably already knows that!" I could hear myself growing hysterical, but I couldn't keep the panic at bay.

"And where do you think you're going to go, Marian? Home?" Addison asked, incredulous.

I paused, willing my breathing to slow. She had a point. If James was the killer and the police hadn't collected enough evidence to bring him in, which was likely considering we were still suspects, chances are he could try to kill me again tonight when I was weakened and vulnerable, alone in my apartment.

"She'll come home with me," Rory said decidedly. We all looked at him in surprise. "What?" he asked, defensively. "I have a spare room. I have a secured entry. I have added a lot of locks onto my door."

Out of the corner of my eye, I saw Addison seem to nod agreeably. I found this odd as she and I had been to Rory's loft only once, despite our years of friendship, and I could barely remember how to get to it, let alone what it looked like. Perhaps I needed an MRI more than I thought.

Rory hopped out of the back of the ambulance, then held

out his arms and gingerly lifted me out and set me on the ground. "Thanks," I said as I wobbled unsteadily.

With a smile, he latched an arm around my waist and turned to Addison. "You coming?" he asked her.

She scurried out of the back of the ambulance and rushed to my other side, helping to prop me up. We had only made it a few steps when she paused and called over her shoulder to Barry, "I have the recording that goes with that pin if you want it. You know where to find me."

As we walked towards Rory's SUV, a detective made his way over to us quickly. "I'll need to ask you all a few questions," he said, apologetically.

Addison shook her head. "You can connect with us tomorrow," she said firmly, continuing to walk me to Rory's suburban.

"It's actually rather important that we speak now," he told her.

Addison sighed and, slowly, she and Rory turned me to face the officer, whom I gave a weak smile. "Does she look like she's in any condition to answer your questions?"

The officer shuffled and flipped to a fresh page in his notebook. "No, but-"

"Do you have any intention of arresting her this evening?" Addison continued, all business.

"No," the officer replied.

"Then you may ask her your questions tomorrow," Addison said firmly. "And Rory and I weren't even around when the explosion happened, so that saves you some time with questioning us."

With that, she and Rory turned me back around slowly and continued to walk me to Rory's SUV.

When I was tucked safely in the backseat, I allowed myself to relax slightly, loosening my stiff muscles as Rory and Addison went around to the other side. Just as I let out a sigh of relief, my door opened. "What did you forget?" I asked, turning with a tired smile. James stood there anxiously and I froze, hearing Addison charging back around to my side of the car, screaming expletives.

"Marian, I'm so sorry," James told me, just before Addison shoved her body between us.

"Sorry that your little plot didn't pan out?" Addison spat, moving forward and forcing him to take a step back. She closed the door behind her and I quickly reached for the lock, clicking it into place as I stared at the pair through my window. James, head lowered like a lost puppy, eventually turned and began walking back towards the dwindling crowd of officers. I lost him when he turned next to a fire truck.

Once he was out of sight, Addison relaxed and walked back around the SUV, opened the rear passenger door and climbed in next to me. Rory closed it softly behind her before hopping into the front. He paused before connecting the key to the ignition and turning the engine over. When his car roared to life without incident, the three of us sighed in relief. I laid my head in Addison's lap and she gingerly began to stroke my head. "Don't fall asleep

yet," she murmured soothingly. "We'll need to keep you
awake for a few hours to make sure everything is okay."

"I'm fine," I mumbled.

"Just a few hours, Marian," Rory repeated, glancing at
us in the rearview mirror. "Just enough time to fill me in on
everything that happened tonight."

Drawing hard from memory, I filled him in on everything
he'd missed, with Addison adding additional commentary
on our drive through the dark streets. Once we arrived at
his apartment, Rory let out a low whistle. "So we're pretty
sure James did it?" he asked, putting his vehicle into park
and turning around to face us.

"I don't mean to put all of our eggs in one basket,"
Addison told him, glancing down at me as I struggled to
fight off the urge to sleep for the next 15 years. My entire
body ached. "But at this particular moment, I have no idea
who else it could be. Even Barry couldn't crack it. And
he's a cop."

Rory allowed her statement to process and then nodded.
"It makes sense," he agreed. "Still, we need to stay alert for
other possibilities."

We made it to Rory's apartment in relative silence, save
for the occasional gasp of pain or grumble from me. My
head continued to feel like it weighed a million pounds and
throbbed with pain. Once my friends had me situated in
Rory's brown leather recliner, Addison made her way
around the corner into what I could only assume was the
bathroom. "Do you have any Advil?" she called out to

Rory, as I heard cabinets opening and closing.

"Bottom drawer," Rory called back to her. Then to me he added, "And I'm going to go fetch you a glass of water."

My pain meds taken, we decided to rent an action film on Rory's slightly large but still incredibly moderate television that hung from his wall. "Anything loud enough to keep you awake," he said, clicking through titles until he found something with my favorite actor in the lead.

He and Addison sat on opposite sides of the loveseat and took turns getting up to come check to make sure I hadn't fallen asleep. Every once in a while, one of them would ask me a stupid question like, "Hey, Marian, what is two plus two?" and I'd snarl in response as I craned my neck around to catch a glimpse of Bruce Willis as he pulled people out of crumbling buildings and led high speed car chases.

When the first movie ended, we ordered another, along with Chinese, my go to comfort food. While I wasn't incredibly hungry — a first — my stomach rolled with nothing more than pain relievers and water, and I knew I'd have no choice but to choke down a spring roll.

Somewhere in the middle of our third movie that night, I found myself nodding off to sleep. When no one came over to gently shake me awake, I curled up even tighter in my blankets, rocked the recliner backward and allowed myself to be lulled into dark, troubled dreams amidst the sound of gunfire popping out of Rory's surround sound speakers.

The next morning, I awoke with a slight crick in my neck, the sun reflecting brightly through the windows. Too brightly. "It snowed!" Addison chirped excitedly behind me. Squatting next to the recliner, she handed me a mug filled with rich black coffee, along with two capsules. "Drink up."

Popping the pain relievers, I blinked hard at the bright sun. "Where am I?" I asked, the night before a complete blur. Rory walked around the corner, swathed in a large bath towel, his chest slightly damp from the shower, his moppy curls shellacked to his head. Suddenly everything came rushing back. "My car," I moaned, covering my eyes with my free hand.

"We can replace that," Addison soothed. "Oh, and your mother called."

"What?" I asked with a start. "She couldn't possibly know-"

"She's your mother. She knows everything," Addison replied, patting my shoulder as she stood and began walking back towards the kitchen. "How about some breakfast? Eggs? Bacon?"

"You sure have made yourself at home," I told her, forcing the recliner upright and standing with a slight wobble. Rory grinned and disappeared into the hall as I followed Addison into the kitchen. "Eggs," I told her. "Scrambled. With cheese. And some toast."

"Anything else?" she asked, nose buried deep in the refrigerator.

"Nope!" I replied cheerfully. After a few moments, I reached for my phone, which sat discarded on the kitchen counter. Checking the battery life, I noted that I still had 39%, which was unfortunately plenty with which to call my mother. Chances are if I didn't reach out soon, she'd call again or simply make the drive down to the city and wait for me at my apartment. I shuddered at the thought. Typing in my pass code, I went to type in her number when the screen lit up with an incoming call. Laughing, I showed it to Addison, who just shook her head as she continued to crack eggs into a large bowl. "Hi, Ma," I said, answering with the speakerphone feature.

"Marian!" my mother cried out. Then, "Don! I have her! She answered! She's alive!"

There were heavy footsteps on the linoleum and then my father's voice echoed through the line. "MnM?" he asked me, using my nickname. "That you?"

"Hi-a, Pop," I whispered.

"Honey, we want you to come stay with us until this is over," my father said loudly into the phone.

"I can't do that," I said simply. "Someone is out to get me and I need to know why."

"What do you mean you need to know why?" my mother

squawked loudly. "Isn't the fact that someone is trying to kill you enough for you? Really. Kids these days."

I sighed, not entirely sure how to explain. "It's someone that I know," I told them. "But I'm still a suspect."

"You're a suspect in your own attempted murder?" my mother cried out. "That's preposterous! Who is this new Captain? I'm going to march myself down there this morning and-"

"It's not just that," I told her. "And how did you know about all of this anyway?"

"It's all over the news," my dad told me. "Porn Maker's Car Goes Up in Flames."

Addison rolled her eyes. "That's not the headline," she mouthed and I grinned.

"Anyway," I said, taking a deep breath, "I need to stay here. And I need you," I paused, "I need both of you to stay there until I get all of this figured out."

I could almost hear my mother arguing with herself over my request but, eventually, she offered a surly, "If you say so," before filling me in on a few updates and hanging up.

"She seems unusually feisty this morning," Addie said as she poured several well-beaten eggs into the hot frying pan. They popped and sizzled as she added various pinches of spice.

"I really hope she doesn't try to get involved," I muttered, dropping my phone to the counter. Sitting up straighter in my chair, I reached for a glass cabinet door and swung it towards me, trying to catch a glimpse of my nasty gash.

"Eesh," I said.

"Pretty nasty," Addie agreed, flipping the eggs with a spatula.

"Thanks," I replied, sarcastically. "Luckily I don't have anything too important on the agenda for today. Wait. Oh, no."

"What?" Addie asked distracted, adding a huge handful of cheese to the eggs.

"My date!" I moaned, clutching my face in my hands. "My date with Mika is tonight. He can't see me looking like this!"

Addie continued to ease the eggs into a scramble, looking anything but flustered. "We'll take care of it," she promised. "I'll help you. But first, I promised to take you down to the police department for questioning at some point this morning."

Just then, Rory stepped out of his room. His hair was still wet but he'd managed to dress in wrinkly cargo pants and a long sleeve shirt, his glasses perched firmly atop his nose. "Breakfast!" he cried, sniffing the air heartily. As he passed me, he gave me a gentle shoulder squeeze. Moving next to Addie, he began to gather plates, cutlery and juice glasses. "Just making yourself right at home then, are you?" he asked her, moving to set things up on the breakfast bar.

Addie flipped the heat to low and pulled a loaf of wheat from the bread basket. Popping two slices into the toaster, she turned back to Rory and gave him a smug smile. "If that's what you'd like to call it," she retorted.

After breakfast, the three of us piled into Rory's SUV and headed over to the police department for questioning. I offered up everything leading up to the explosion, including my date. However, I left out the piece about catching everything on tape figuring I'd save that tidbit for later use, if needed.

After questioning, Rory dropped Addison and I at the office, where we picked up her car. Mine was no longer in the lot but there was quite a bit of scorching left in its place. Once we'd determined that the coast was clear in my apartment, she left me to relax and get cleaned up, promising to return later that day to help me get ready.

After quieting my hungry stomach with half a can of Pringles, I popped a few more pain relievers and checked the clock. There were at least three hours to kill and that was only if I planned on taking over two hours to get ready. Numbly, I caught sight of my Swiffer. May as well clean the apartment. It's not like I could really go anywhere.

Three and a half hours later, my apartment, including Fred's tank, was spotless. Additionally, all of my laundry had been washed and folded, neatly tucked into various drawers and closets. Lost in the smell of Pine Sol, I was shaken back to reality by a loud knock on my door. "Are you in there?" Addie shouted. When I opened the door, her arms were overflowing with dry cleaning bags. She looked me up and down in horror. "Why haven't you showered yet?"

"I've been cleaning," I replied. "Besides, who needs over two hours to get ready?"

She pointed to the ugly gash on my forehead. "That does." Shooing me to the shower, she carried her dry cleaning down to the bedroom.

Twenty five minutes of tender soaping and rinsing later, I was wrapped in a warm, fluffy towel, sitting on my bed. Addie buzzed around me, checking the various brushes and heated contraptions she'd brought with her as she ran through the outfits she'd laid out for me. "This one," she said, picking up a low-cut red satin dress, "is something you can wear if you're worried about his eyes wandering. He won't be able to get enough of you."

I made a face and shook my head. While I didn't consider myself to be remotely in the same hotness realm as Mika, I wasn't too worried about his ability to remain focused. Plus, the dress practically screamed "do me," which I wasn't ready for just yet.

Addie hurried over to a ruffled blouse and knee-length purple pencil skirt. "This one looks like you've been at the office all day. Sexy young professional."

I shook my head again. I didn't want to give the impression that I always dressed up for work. He'd seen me in cute professional gear only the day before. Twice in a row, for someone who usually showed up in jeans or yoga gear, would give the wrong impression.

Addie picked up the last outfit she had laid out. Black

skinny jeans paired with a loose gray V-neck sweater.

"That's it," I breathed, reaching out to finger the soft cashmere. "Where did you find this?"

"Never you mind," she was grinning. "You can keep it. Consider it a gift." She let the words "I'm glad you're not dead" prior to "gift" be assumed.

A few minutes later, I was snug in my new outfit, sitting perfectly still as Addie fussed with my curls with a hair diffuser and a can of hairspray. "How do you feel about bangs?" she asked, eyeing me critically once my hair was dry. "Maybe something side swept." She tried tucking a mass of curls over my gash, critiquing the potential outcome.

"I'm not sure," I responded nervously as Addison chewed her lower lip, eying me. "Can't you just try to cover up the bruising with makeup?"

Gritting her teeth, she gingerly tapped the bruising around my cut. "Yeow!" I howled, batting her hands away. "Why did you do that?"

"To show you that I won't be able to get anywhere near that cut with a makeup sponge," she chided. "Where are your scissors?"

"Kitchen junk drawer." As she went in search of them, I surveyed the mess that was scattered across my dresser, nightstand and floor. Makeup. Clothes. Bags. Hair tools. Shoes. What a good friend I had in Addison Dawes.

Addie returned and took a small handful of my hair in her fist. Picking up her straightener, she began to iron out the curls until she held a thick, straight curtain of dark hair. Slowly, cautiously, she snipped. After a few moments, she swept the straightened hair to the side pinning it into place, stepped back and surveyed her work. "Not bad," she muttered, passing me a handheld mirror. I gasped. She'd managed to completely cover the gash and surrounding bruise under an adorable patch of bangs. "Now for makeup," she said, taking the mirror and setting it behind her.

By the time Addison had finished, I appeared more put together than I probably had in weeks. She'd paired my outfit with a pair of gray leather boots that had been sitting untouched in my closet for over a year. Additionally, she'd chosen a pair of silver hoop earrings and a matching bracelet from my jewelry box. Even my makeup looked flawless, despite the abrupt end to it right around the bruising. Together, we packed up all of her belongings and carried them down to her car before she dropped me off at the warehouse. "Call me if you need a ride," she said, kissing me lightly on the cheek. "Actually, just call me when you get home, no matter what."

I waved goodbye to her at the door and let myself inside to wait. Someone had removed the black curtain and I found myself hugging my body as I walked through the studio, my footsteps echoing off the walls. I was so engrossed that I didn't hear anyone walk in.

"Wow," Rory said, appreciatively adding a low whistle. "You look fantastic." He gave me a twirl motion with his finger and I obligingly spun in a slow circle. "Hot date?" he asked.

"Who should be meeting me here at any moment," I responded.

Just then, the main door opened and Mika stepped in. Rory raised his eyebrows at me, wiggled them in a suggestive fashion, grinning as he walked back towards the admin wing. "Let me know if you need a ride later," he called over his shoulder.

I chucked and walked towards Mika. "Hi," I said shyly, unsure of what to do.

He flashed me his crooked smile and I about died on the spot. "Hi," he responded. "Marian, you look…wow."

"Thanks," I replied shyly suddenly aware of nothing other than the pounding of my heart.

He reached out for my hand and held it even as he opened the door. Once on the street, we began walking towards the main hub of downtown. "I'd drive us, but it's probably just as easy to walk now that the sidewalks have been cleared of snow. Plus, it makes for a longer conversation."

"Unless the conversation is uncomfortable, in which case, we'll both have wished you'd driven," I teased back, surprised at how natural the flirting felt.

He laughed. "I don't think that's going to be a problem," he said, squeezing my hand gently. "Well, look, I didn't make a reservation. I decided that we could just go with what we felt like and if it's a long wait, we just have that much longer to get to know one another."

"Sounds great," I smiled. My stomach growled in disagreement, but I ignored it.

We decided on a restaurant situated on the riverfront, lucking into a window table when our names were called. Mika and I lingered over wine and appetizers, laughing heartily and playing off of the other in conversation. It was like a meal between long lost friends. I felt as if I'd known him forever.

After dinner, and better still, cheesecake for dessert, we walked along the riverfront for a short time before finally bowing to the cold and snow. Hurrying our way back down to the warehouse, we gripped hands tightly, pulling one another along against the wind.

The office was empty, lights turned off. I unlocked the doors and Mika and I ducked inside, laughing. "I had a great time," he told me after our giggles had subsided.

"I did too," I replied honestly.

"Again, then, Marian. Soon," he said.

I could only nod. Would he kiss me? I wasn't sure. I found myself getting lost in his bright blue eyes and leaned back against the door for support, ignoring the chill that crept through my sweater. I noticed that while he had retrieved his keys from his pocket, he was only fiddling with them and didn't seem in much of a hurry to get out the door. I swallowed. It had been a considerable amount of time since a man looked at me in the way Mika was looking at me now. While I didn't want to give him the wrong impression, I also wanted whatever he was prepared to offer in that moment. And what was wrong with that? I owed this to myself. Especially considering everything I'd been through in the last 24 hours. Besides, I was showered and had actually bothered to shave my legs this afternoon — a feat I hadn't attempted since summer, from what it looked like. Plus Mika could just as soon dump me after our first date as our 50th.

Mika seemed to be thinking along the same lines, because he was moving closer. Our eyes remained locked as he drew near. My palms began to sweat. My breath probably wasn't the greatest. I hadn't kissed anyone in about three years either. This had potential disaster written all over it. Additionally, my hair was starting to wilt. I brushed it out of my eyes and licked my lips in anticipation. He stopped. "Marian!" he cried in surprise, leaping the last few feet to my side. He gently starting combing my straightened bangs off of my forehead and I instantly realized what I'd done.

"Oh no," I moaned, combing everything back into place with my fingertips. "It's fine, it's fine, just leave it."

"Marian, what happened?"

"I just had a little…accident. It's no big deal."

"You look like you smashed your head on the concrete." We stared at one another long and hard. "You're telling me you actually smashed your head on the concrete?"

"Something like that."

"Go on."

"It's nothing. It's just that my car exploded yesterday and it's possible that someone is trying to kill me, but it's probably not a big deal and it's really nothing you should worry about." I paused. "But maybe we shouldn't eat the baked goods from any further photo shoots until everything settles down a bit," I added.

He seemed to take all of this in stride, but something seemed to dawn on him as he watched me. "Your car exploded?" he asked. "How were you going to get home tonight?"

"I guess I was having such a great time that I forgot about that. I can just call Addie."

"Absolutely not. I'm happy to give you a ride home."

"Oh, you don't have to-"

"Marian? Shut up and get in the truck."

As it turned out, Mika owned a Jeep that was the same deep blue as his eyes. I briefly wondered if that had been intentional. I liked a Jeep on a man. Good, rugged vehicle. Even better was that it housed a black leather interior with seat warmers. When Mika pulled to a stop in front of my building, I paused before exiting, wondering if there was any hope of rekindling the magic that we'd cast back at the studio. As it turned out, I needn't have worried. "I'd like to kiss you," he said, leaning forward and touching his palm to my cheek. "If that would be okay."

Addie had told me earlier that day that Mika looked like the kind of man who knew what he was doing. "Really attractive men are usually atrocious in the bedroom," she'd said as she straightened my hair. "They think it's enough to just look good." I believed her because she'd been with her fair share of incredibly attractive men. "But there's something about that one. Something that makes me think he can blow your mind."

Up until this moment, I wasn't totally sure what I was expecting. Nothing like what would follow. He wrapped his free hand in the hair at the base of my skull and gently held me there as he moved in to kiss my chin, my jaw and even my neck. I allowed my eyes to flutter closed as he trailed soft licks and kisses down my collarbone. Without warning, he pressed his lips softly to mine and loosened his hand in my hair, allowing me to sink into him. Our tongues touched and the kiss grew deeper. My entire body immediately morphed into jelly and I thanked my lucky stars that I hadn't received this kiss while standing.

When it was over, I was frozen in place with my eyes still closed. After a few seconds, I blinked them open. Mika was smiling back at me. Grinning, I reached for the door handle and managed to get it open on my third attempt. Rattled, I tried stepping out of the Jeep only to realize that I was still buckled in. Laughing nervously, I unstrapped the harness and all but fell out of the car, catching myself on the door. "Careful, it's pretty slippery out here," I told him, slamming the door closed behind me and walking as quickly as possible to the lobby of my building.

Once inside, I turned to wave and it wasn't until I got to the elevator that the full weight of what had just happened sunk in. Somewhere around the fourth floor, I completely lost it. Somewhere around the eighth floor, I was back in moderate control. By the time the elevator doors zinged open on my floor, I was a picture of calm. Floating to my door, I inserted my key into the lock and turned it. Nothing happened. The door was already unlocked.

I paused, trying to think back to earlier in the day when
Addison and I left, our hands full of items she was taking
home with her. Had I remembered to lock the door behind
me? Frantically, I began tracing my steps back through the
evening. I had, in fact, remembered to lock both the knob
and the deadbolt, I recalled, because I'd made Addison
take all of my bags as I searched for my keys to do so.
My heart was pounding in my chest as I slowly removed
the key from the lock. Taking a step backwards, I tried to
take a deep, calming breath. I wasn't sure what to do. I
could go downstairs, but I didn't have a car. I could just go
inside, but I ran the risk of interrupting whatever was
happening. Chances were it wasn't just a random break-in
as there were no signs of forced entry. Making my way
slowly towards the stairwell, I started to dig around for my
phone. I could call 911. Granted, I was already on thin ice
as it was. Still, it's better to be safe than sorry. Chances
were that whoever got sent out to check my place at this
hour wasn't going to be anyone I'd interacted with before.
Maybe they wouldn't recognize me.

About halfway down the first staircase, I pressed the
emergency call button on my phone. "9-1-1, what's your
emergency?" asked a bored voice.

"Someone broke into my apartment," I hissed, looking up to make sure that I wasn't being followed.

"Okay, ma'am, are you currently in your apartment?"

"No, I'm heading down to the lobby."

"What's your address?" I rattled it off and she repeated it back to me. Once I confirmed, she promised that units were on their way, before asking, "Was your door open? Or how did you know that someone had broken in?"

"The door was unlocked."

There was a pause on the other end of the line and the clicking of her keyboard stopped. "I'm sorry?" she asked.

"The door was unlocked," I repeated. "I distinctly recall locking it when I left this evening. When I put in my key to unlock it when I got back, it was already unlocked."

"Were there any signs of forced entry?" she asked, and the typing picked up again.

"No," I sighed. "Look. I know this sounds crazy, but I think someone is trying to kill me. First the cupcakes, then the car and now they're just going to handle it themselves." When there was no response, I sighed again. "You're sure someone is on the way?"

"Yes, ma'am. Please just stay on the line with me until they arrive."

"That's fine," I told her. "I'm in the lobby, now. I'll just wait."

"Ma'am, I'm happy to-"

"Thanks," I said, cutting her off and clicking off the call. Hugging myself, I leaned against one of the whitewashed walls in the lobby and caught my reflection in a mirror that resembled a sunburst. I looked pretty good, save for the weariness that was evident in my eyes. Blowing my loose bangs out of my eyes, I turned towards the main doors of the lobby and waited. Hopefully someone from the police department arrived before whoever was upstairs made it down here. Wasn't there a statistic that chances were whoever was trying to kill you was someone you knew?

Over the next ten minutes, the elevator dinged itself open a total of seven times, which is about the number of coronaries I experienced. Would I recognize the person who stepped off?

I continually checked my watch, paced the lobby and looked outside, hoping that the emergency operator hadn't changed her mind and called off the squad because I'd hung up on her. She wasn't allowed to do that, was she? If you are under the impression that ten minutes doesn't feel like a lifetime, I'm sorry to say that you're incorrect.

When a squad car finally parked in front of my building, I pulled tightly at my jacket and ran outside. The lights on the car weren't flashing, but whoever it was had been clipping along at a pretty good speed and was forced to come to an abrupt stop. The driver side door opened as I waited in front of my building, hopping from one foot to the other, trying desperately to stay warm.

"Hey Marian!" said the man who stepped out of the vehicle.

Wonderful. Now I was going to look like a spastic idiot

143

in front of someone that knew exactly who I was. Wait a second. Was that- "Barry?" I asked, squinting through the cold windy darkness.

"That's my name!"

"What are you doing over here? This neighborhood isn't anywhere near your beat."

"I recognized your address when the call came over the radio. Seeing as how you've had all kinds of problems lately, I assumed you had made the call. Thought I'd pop over and see if I could be of any help."

"I think someone is in my apartment," I said, trailing him inside and over to the elevator. "I locked my door when I left today and when I got home, it was unlocked." Barry fixed me with a look as we rode up to my floor. "I know I sound crazy, but it's true!" I promised, throwing my hands in the air. I was tired of sounding crazy.

"Did you ever get that gun?" he asked, turning down the radio speaker that was attached to his uniform.

"Yes."

"Well where is it?"

"In my sock drawer."

Barry snorted. "Fat lot of good it does you in there."

When we stopped on my floor, Barry made a "stay behind me" motion as he crept towards the door. His hand slowly wrapped around his gun, which he pulled quietly from its holster. Very slowly, he twisted the doorknob, pushing the door wide open and raised his gun towards my living room. It was completely black save for the moonlight that shown in through the windows. "Light switch?" he whispered, not bothering to lower his weapon. I thought it an odd question, considering the panel was in clear view just ahead, but maybe he wasn't paying attention to that. "Left side," I answered.

Still holding tightly to his gun with his right hand, Barry stepped in and flipped on the lights. "Wait here," he told me as he continued inside the apartment. Hugging myself tightly, I waited just outside, straining to hear for any loud thuds or shouts, but none came. "Coast is clear," he told me finally, coming around the corner and holstering his gun. "But you're right about one thing. Someone was definitely in here. It looks like they were interrupted, though." He checked my locks carefully, searching for signs of forced entry.

Pushing past him, I ran my eyes over the living room, which was completely torn to bits. Pillows and blankets were everywhere, my couch cushions were overturned and all of the drawers to my entertainment center stood open, like a slack-jawed idiot, befuddled that it had been violated so harshly. The rug that was under the couch had been thrown back as if someone had been looking for trick floorboards. My bedroom was much of the same. The bed was a mess, my dresser ransacked with clothes thrown all over the place. My nightstand however, remained untouched. Hurrying over, I pulled open the second drawer, where my gun was still safely stashed inside a large pair of fluffy pink socks. Breathing a sigh of relief, I tucked it, sock and all, into my purse and quietly closed the drawer.

When I stepped back into the living room, Barry was calling for backup. Stepping over to Fred's tank, I dropped in a small pinch of food. He went after the flakes with vigor. "I'll give you more if you can tell me who was in here," I promised, tapping lightly on his bowl. He ignored my offer and continued to eat the food that came without strings attached. Sighing, I turned back to Barry. "So what do I do now?" I asked.

"First we wait. Then, honestly? I'd recommend you find a place to crash for a few days."

What a crock. I was being chased out of my own home. Despite the problems, it was still my haven. I hated the idea of living elsewhere, if only until the robber was caught. Who knew how long that would take? Besides, there was a chance it was all a big coincidence, right? That the robber and the killer were not one in the same? "I'll be in the hall," I muttered. Outside my apartment, I hastily dialed the first number that came to mind. Addison.

"Ohmigawwwwd," she squealed, picking up on the first ring. "I've been waiting for you to call. How was the date?"

"I'm home."

She gasped. "Is he there with you? I can't believe you already brought him upstairs! That is totally a page torn straight from my personal book of life. How is he? Is he as good as I thought he'd be? Better? Like, way better?"

"Addie, I need a ride."

"Well, get off the phone and go get one! Why are you still talking to me?"

"No, Addison. He's not at my place. He dropped me off. But someone broke into my apartment."

I heard her phone clatter to the floor. "I'll be right there," she hollered and then the line went dead.

Thirty minutes later, I was giving yet another statement to the police when Addison came barreling out of the elevator. "Out of my way," she growled, shoving her way through the small throng of personnel that now littered the hallway. Most of them were neighborhood gawkers, but there were a few police and crime investigators that were milling near my front door. And what a sight Addison was. Her normal sleek locks were gnarled rat nests that gave her a slightly homeless appearance. Her eyes were bright and wild, red lipstick slightly smudged. To top it off, she was practically swimming in a large fur coat that clearly wasn't hers. "Where is she?" she called, glancing around the apartment. When we locked eyes, she stalked over to my side and threw her arms around my neck. "Are you alright?"

"I'm fine," I promised. Gently shoving her away, I pointed to her coat. "That thing stinks. Like a 90 year old woman died in it."

"Close, I'm told that she was 93."

"Who does that even belong to?"

"Rory's grandmother," she answered nonchalantly.

That wasn't the answer I was expecting. Perhaps in my

tired, crazy haze I'd hallucinated. "Why the hell do you have Rory's grandmother's fur coat?"

"I was in a rush. I couldn't find my jacket."

"So Rory invited you to take his dead grandmother's coat? Which, for some reason, he kept stored at our office?"

"His apartment."

"What the hell were you doing at Rory's apartment?"

"Can we talk about this later, 20 Questions? Your night has clearly been more eventful."

I scanned suspiciously over her ratty hair and smudged lipstick. With a gasp I shouted, "You're sleeping with Rory!"

The entire room went silent as everyone turned to look at us. The detective who had been questioning me cleared his throat awkwardly. "I'm just going to let the two of you talk for a minute-"

"No!" Addison cried. "We're done talking."

"We've so just started talking."

"We're finished."

"For now," I added. She stuck her tongue out at me before sidling up next to Barry as I continued to answer the detective's questions. The chaos that had hushed around us eventually whirred back to full volume.

"I can't believe I interrupted you and Rory having sex," I told Addison once we were sitting inside her car. "When did that happen? How? Why? Oh, God, are you taking me to his apartment?"

"He does have a secure entry."

"Addison!"

"Oh, come on!" she cried. "You're going to have to fill us both in, anyway. Besides, I'd personally feel a lot safer with a guy around. Not that I can't take care of myself."

"Rory doesn't strike me as the protective type. And you're not allowed to have sex while I'm there."

"But-"

"Not. Allowed."

"Fine," she groused as we pulled out onto the main street. We sat in silence as Addie navigated the back roads towards Rory's apartment.

When we were close, I asked, "But really, how long has this been going on?"

Her cheeks grew pink but she kept her eyes on the road. "A while."

"Addie…"

"Since Alec died."

"That's almost three weeks! Peter came out to see you! Peter was in your apartment the day we drove to my parents' house. Oh my God, Rory was Pete. Rory was naked upstairs! That's why you were already waiting for me outside! You were worried I was going to come up to get you and find Rory naked."

"Great, can we change the subject now?"

"You don't want to talk about it? That means it must be serious," I teased. "You always love sharing all the dirty

149

details." She didn't respond and a sobering thought washed over me. "Holy crap, it's serious?"

"Is there something wrong with my being serious about someone?"

"Nope."

"Excellent," she said, staring straight ahead. "Now let's focus on the bigger issue at hand."

"Mika?" I asked hopefully. I felt a flutter in my stomach when I thought of our kiss and closed my eyes, relishing the memory. It seemed like it had happened so long ago when, in fact, it had only been a few hours.

"No, although I want to hear all about that later. Right now I want to know why someone would break into your apartment."

I shrugged and sank back into my seat. "In case you haven't noticed, someone has been trying to kill me off. While I am a young, moderately attractive female, I'm not a virgin. If this were a movie, people would probably be screaming at the screen, telling me I'm next. " I paused, turning to look glumly out the window. When Addison didn't respond, I felt my heart begin to race.

Was I with the killer? Gulping, I continued to let fear prickle at my neck, refusing to make eye contact with her. She continued to say nothing, which only enhanced by heart rate. My circumstances were fairly dire. We were on an interstate. There was no way I could leap out of the vehicle. Addison was one to drive well over posted speed limits. Then again, she knew every cop in town and never seemed to acquire a ticket. No one would pull us over. No one would hear me beg for help. I always figured myself to be the type who could be rather cool in the face of death. I figured wrong.

When I couldn't take the tension any longer, I whispered "Addie?"

"Hmm?" She asked. "Oh, sorry, darling, I was daydreaming. What were you saying?"

The air rushed out of my lungs and tears stung at the corners of my eyes. My throat was growing thick with emotion. I really was going crazy if I thought Addison was out to kill me. "I just said someone is after me" I muttered, embarrassed by my crazy imagination.

"But if they just wanted to kill you, why would they ransack your apartment? Why not just wait until you walk in, shoot you and leave?"

"Maybe someone is trying to shake me up a little bit first. Keep me on my toes."

"Signs of forced entry?"

"Nope. I have that key taped in the top of my door frame."

"Yeah, but the tape blends with the wood so well that only the people you've told would know it was there, right?"

I shrugged. "I thought so. Maybe it's not hidden well, when you consider that someone is a killer for hire, though." I stared glumly out the window. "Once they've messed with me enough, they'll kill me." I looked at my friend sideways and could see that she was thinking hard. "What?" I asked.

She shook her head. "James just doesn't strike me as the type of individual who would do the dirty work."

"You think he has help?"

"Yup. But if killing really is his line of business, the cops can kiss fingerprints and DNA goodbye. We're on our own."

"They can't possibly still think that we're behind this. My apartment was ransacked!"

"Your building doesn't have cameras. Your last sexual escapade was years ago. The only DNA in that apartment will be ours from this afternoon," Addie told me, seriously. "We need to get ahead of the curve on this case because James is about to cross the finish line and we're looking nothing but guilty. It doesn't help that your first responder was Barry."

"I know," I groused. "I didn't ask for that to happen. So what's the plan?"

"I have an idea, but it's not going to make us many friends," she said, pulling off the road into Rory's parking lot.

"I don't really care about making friends right now."

"It could potentially cost you your job with the department."

I sucked in my breath. "Well," I said after a beat, "that might just be the risk I have to take."

True to her word, Addie refrained from sleeping with Rory that night. Then again, I'm a heavy sleeper. Still, I woke up before the sun the next day and was unable to fall back asleep. I tossed and turned on the sofa, eventually flipping on the television. Once the volume was lowered, I channel surfed until settling on my favorite comedy reruns.

When Addison emerged from Rory's bedroom about three hours later, she looked much the way she had when she picked me up the night before. However, she was dressed in only a men's long-sleeve button down and little else. She scratched her head sleepily and yawned a "good morning" my way. "How long have you been awake?"

"Few hours," I told her as she made her way past me. I held up my hand to shield my eyes. "Girl. Put on some pants." She ignored me and began pulling items out of cabinets for coffee. I flipped off the television and moved to a barstool in the kitchen. "Well, if you won't put on pants, are you at least going to fill me in on your plan?"

"Not yet," she said as she filled the coffee pot with water. "I don't want you to have any more information than you absolutely need right now. You're terrible at hiding things."

"Don't remind me."

"And you're even worse at keeping secrets."

"That's true."

"But trust me when I say that I will take good care of you. Okay?"

I took her hand across the counter and smiled. "I know that." How could I have ever thought last night, even for a second, that she was out to get me? This entire experience was making me paranoid. It was turning me against the people that I loved and relied upon most in the world. Perhaps that's what the killer wanted.

"In the meantime, we're back to trying to figure out why you're a target. Your car explodes. Someone breaks into your apartment. We need to figure out what happens next or we may not get another chance."

"There's a cheery thought to start the morning," Rory said as he made his way into the kitchen. "Morning, kiddo," he said, squeezing my shoulder. "Morning, love," he said to Addie, slipping up behind her and brushing her cheek with his lips. Thankfully, he was wearing not only pants, but also a shirt. I loved Rory, but I wasn't ready for him to bare as much as Addison was this morning.

"I still don't understand how this happened," I told them. They smiled at me but said nothing. "Anyway, I know I'm not going to be privy to the plan," I said with a hint of sarcasm. "But is there anything I can do to help in the meantime?"

"Staying alive would be a start," Rory replied, pulling eggs, milk and blueberries out of the refrigerator. "Pancakes?"

"Please."

"So we're sure that James is in on it," Addie mused as she placed three mugs on the counter. "But we're pretty sure someone else is in on it with him."

"Maybe. But given the timeline, he could be the one who rigged up my car," I suggested.

"It's possible but, when that didn't work, why didn't he finish the job of killing you when you were out cold on the sidewalk?" she mused.

"Because in that scenario, the cops could pin the whole thing on him," I supplied. "But for some reason, the cops still think we killed Alec. James knows it. And he's going to use that to his advantage until I'm dead."

"Is he trying to kill all of us or just you? Maybe killing Alec was an accident," Rory offered nonchalantly as he began to whisk ingredients together.

The three of us pondered this possibility for a few moments. Addie poured three mugs of hot coffee and prepared each the way their taker liked. Then she came and sat next to me as Rory poured pancake batter onto the hot griddle. He had all the coolest kitchen gadgets despite the fact that his wardrobe was clearly lacking in latest and greatest. Priorities, I suppose. Men. "We haven't even had a chance to review the bakery," I said, reminded that we hadn't worked on the writing for the bakery project since before Alec had died.

"I don't know how we're going to," Addie said. "I'm not eating what they sent over for this last shoot. They probably doubled the arsenic in the second batch. No way. If I can't see where it has been, it's not going in my mouth." She took a sip of her coffee as Rory and I snickered. "Real mature," she murmured into her mug. "That's not what I meant."

"Wait a second!" I shouted, slamming my hand on the counter in eureka. "Maybe James really is the hit man!"

"You've got to be kidding," Addie responded. "I was just joking about that last night. He couldn't be. He's too attractive. It's such a dirty line of business. Plus, he'd own it, not be it. Don't you think?" Rory just flipped the pancakes and looked at us both quizzically. Still, my brain was alive, wrapping itself around the possibility.

"Exactly! It makes sense!" I told them both eagerly. "James suggested that he was in a shady line of business. We've determined that he has a partner. What if James is just the puppet master who ultimately takes the orders and passes them down to his man? He doesn't need a reason to kill people, he just needs someone else who does. He makes a lot of money doing the dirty work for other people."

"Then he creates a plausible scenario," Addie added.

"And whoever his assistant is pulls it off!" I finished.

"So we were all supposed to die," Rory said, placing a plate of blueberry pancakes in front of us. Addie stood to retrieve syrup and butter as Rory counted out plates and cutlery.

"Poisoning the food of the food critics," I mused. "The only question is, out of all the people you and I have pissed off, who would be angry enough to try to kill us?"

"I'd start with the places that have shut down following a negative review," said Rory.

"Great idea," Addie replied, nodding. "Marian, do you have access to our full list of clients?" I nodded. "Great. After breakfast, we're going to start comparing those against a list of who is no longer in business." She rubbed her hands together gleefully. "Maybe we won't have to execute my original plan after all."

Following breakfast, Addie and Rory went to go use the shower in his master suite. Meanwhile, I locked the door to his guest bath and showered all by myself. Relaxing my tense shoulders under the spray of warm water I tried desperately to turn off my busy mind.

Dressed in a slightly too busty outfit Addie had loaned me from her overnight bag, I went to clean up the kitchen. I had just begun to wipe down the countertops when Addison and Rory stepped out of the bedroom, hanging all over one another like lovesick teenagers. I'd never seen Addie so into a guy. Sure, she and Peter had made a movie star quality couple but, while she'd loved him, it never seemed like she relied on him for much outside of the obvious.

The three of us piled into Rory's SUV and we made our way slowly to the warehouse. It had snowed again the night before and the roads weren't fully plowed. Traffic crept along slowly and the three of us maintained cheerful chatter about everything except our potential demise.

We entered the office through the back alley and greeted Betsy, who simply nodded to us in acknowledgement. "She's coming up on the end of her quarter," Addie muttered as we walked up the stairs to the main office. "After that she's gone."

"Any chance of getting her out of here prior to Thanksgiving?"

"No shot."

I sighed. "After all this is over, remind me to look over her application so that I know exactly what not to choose for spring."

Upstairs, Addie checked messages as I turned on my computer and waited for it to buzz to life. Once I was logged in, she handed me a yellow sticky note. "Think you can return these calls today? I have to run to the Journal."

"It's Sunday," I protested. "I thought you were going to help me compare lists."

"There's something I need to do there while it's quiet," she told me, hitching up her purse. "I'm going to take Rory. Can you hold down the fort for a little while?"

"I guess," I grumbled.

She gave me an awkward hug promising to lock me in and then raced out the door. Sighing, I pulled up the list from our database of every business *Food Porn* had ever reviewed. It was longer than I'd thought. Pulling it to one side of my computer screen, I brought up a search engine and painstakingly began to research every single one of them. If the place was still open, I made a note of it. If the place had closed, I made a note of it. If the place re-opened or if the owner had gone on to own another business, I made note of that, too.

I was so lost in my research that I didn't notice when Addie walked in carrying a gorgeous vase filled with huge white lilies. Nearly falling out of my chair when she plunked them down on the table next to me, I moved my hand to my chest. "Jesus," I panted. "You scared me half to death."

"Sorry. Rory and I just got back and there was a delivery guy from the florist shop out front. These are for you but I went ahead and signed for them."

"Who are they from?" I asked suspiciously.

She shrugged. "I have no idea. But chances are good that they're from someone still reeling from a hot date last night."

Finally locating the card, which was tucked deep in the bouquet, I pulled it out with a flourish. "Maybe you're right," I told her with a grin. I paused, taking a moment to indulge in their beautiful scene before ripping into the envelope and yanking out the card.

"Eager, are we?" Addie teased.

I read the cursive black scrawl on the plain white card. Blinking hard, I squinted and read it again. Suddenly, the room around me went hazy and I felt blood pounding in my ears as I struggled to breathe. I dropped the card as though it were on fire and pushed myself roughly out of

159

my chair. Backing away from the desk, I pressed myself against the cool window and felt a sob rising in my throat as hot tears stung my eyes.

"Breathe," Addie was saying. It was as if I were hearing her voice from underwater. "In through your nose, out through your mouth." I felt my knees giving out and sank heavily to the floor, where I curled my arms around my knees and quietly began to rock back and forth.

Addie was rubbing my back and screaming for Rory, who came barreling into the office holding his gun. "What the hell are you doing?" she cried when she saw it.

"I thought you were in danger."

"Get that thing out of here," she cried, waving her arms frantically.

"What the hell is going on?"

"I don't know. I just brought her the flowers. We thought they were from Mika but she opened the card and started freaking out."

"What's the card say?" Rory asked, stepping closer.

"I don't know! It's over there," and she pointed to the other side of my desk. Rory gingerly reached for the card as Addie continued to rub my back. My head was pounding. After reading the note, Rory cast us a worried glance before reading it again. "Well?" Addison begged impatiently. "What's going on? What does it say?"

Rory swallowed hard and handed the card to Addie. After reading it, her hand flew to her mouth. "I can't believe this."

160

After a moment's pause, she and Rory wrapped me in a tight hug. I'm not sure how long we stayed there, but out of the corner of my eye I could just barely make out the words that had been sent as a message along with my beautiful bouquet.

Dear Marian. These were for your funeral. I'd hate to see them go to waste. XO

Betsy walked in and looked at the three of us huddled together on the floor. "What's going on?" she asked. "I heard screaming and then I saw Rory running upstairs with a gun." She paused. "Please tell me you didn't find another body."

"Nothing like that," said Rory, clearing his throat and then standing. "We just thought that-"

"False alarm," Addison cut him off. She, too, stood and moved next to Rory. He turned to her, confused, but didn't say anything further. "It's okay though, Betsy, you can go back to work."

I could feel Betsy cut her eyes to me. I was still huddled into a ball on the floor, my forehead pressed tightly against my knees. All I could see were their shoes. Rory's sensible brown loafers. Betsy's furry, black boots. Addie's sky-high red heels. Betsy wanted to say something to me, obvious by the way she hesitated, but eventually she turned and made her way to the door, where she paused. I heard her take a deep breath and I raised my head, watching her. She was searching the room. When her eyes landed on the flowers, she wrinkled her nose. We locked eyes and, I swear, my heart stopped beating when I saw the ice in her gaze. "Smells like a funeral parlor," she scoffed. With that, she turned and made her way back down the stairs.

The room around me became devoid of air. "How did she-?" I asked.

Rory was staring after her, slack-jawed. "What did she just say?" Addie demanded.

"Did you say that you met the florist at the front door when you came back?" I looked to Rory, then to Addie, then back to Rory. "Isn't that what you told me?" I shrieked when neither one of them responded.

"Yes! I'm sorry. Yes," Addie blurted out. "He said he hadn't gotten anyone to answer the door."

"But Betsy was here," I said, confused. "She just told us that she heard screaming and then saw Rory running upstairs with a gun. Why wouldn't she answer the door?"

Addison turned to me, her eyes wide. "Maybe she just got here. You don't think that she- I mean, Betsy isn't capable of- why would she?"

I stared back at her, speechless. Without warning, I felt hysterical laughter bubbling up in my throat. I couldn't help it. I began to laugh so hard that I clutched at my stomach, tears rolling down the sides of my face.

"She's lost it," Addison mumbled, coming to sit down next to me. Slowly, my laughter turned into wrenching sobs. Between wails I gasped for air, laying my head heavily onto Addison's shoulder.

"Okay, let's not lose total focus here," Rory said, beginning to pace the room.

"He's not very comfortable around women who cry"

Addison told me. I could only wail louder, unsure of how to reign in my emotions. She looked to Rory apologetically but could only shrug at him.

Rory continued to pace, cringing slightly each time a new cry ripped from my throat. "Just a few hours ago, we were convinced it was James. Now we're looking at Betsy?" He jammed his thumb towards the door. "You think that, that could be a cold blooded killer?" He shook his head. "No. There's no way. She has no reason to kill anyone in this room."

"We turned her down for the modeling gig," Addison said simply.

"After the original murder, though."

"Maybe she was hoping that by getting rid of a model, she could take their place."

"How would she know that a model would eat the food? They never eat the food."

Addison paused. "Maybe she just doesn't like the three of us?"

"Then why kill Alec?"

"It could have been an accident."

"You're crazy."

"I'm just trying to consider every possibility," Addison shot back.

"It was just a stupid, off-the-cuff comment she made," Rory cried. Putting his hands on his hips, he took a deep breath. "Okay," he said. "I think it's fair to say that Marian is having a stressful day." I sniffled in response, my sobs having trickled down to a quiet whimper. "But I also think that if we're being rational about all of this, Betsy simply didn't hear the knock on the door from her cubicle. I think she made an ill-timed comment. However, I do not think that it makes sense that she would murder a male model in an attempt to gain access to the modeling world."

"We can't be rational about this," Addison said. "Nothing about any of this is rational."

"That's true," I finally chimed in, shaky. "But Rory is right, we can't keep jumping to conclusions."

"What if Betsy hired James?" Addison asked, looking back and forth between us. "Did you think about that?"

"Do you have any idea how much a hit man costs?" Rory asked her.

"No. Do you?"

He smiled and ran a hand through his hair. "Touché. But trust me, a college student probably couldn't afford it. And I'm willing to bet that if she'd borrowed the money from her parents, they'd have been less than inclined to assist."

"She could be James's assistant," I murmured. They both turned to stare at me. "Well it kind of makes sense," I went on. "Some crazy restaurateur that we drove out of business wants to kill us. Betsy isn't included because she probably wasn't even working for the magazine at the time the negative review was written. James needs someone we're close to and not suspicious of. He offers her a fistful of cash. It's done."

"She's not even trained to kill," Addison cried out in

disbelief. "She leaves cans and wrappers all over the building, but you think she's capable of wiping down fingerprints?"

"Could be a cover," I muttered.

"If, and only if, this were possible, why take out Alec first?" Addison challenged. I could see the wheels in her head turning as her mind began to weave together a potential story.

"It was probably an accident," I shrugged. "She probably poisoned the cupcakes the night before. For whatever reason, Alec had the munchies and figured he'd catch some grub at the studio. He'd know from past experience that we'd already have the food delivered for our shoot the following day."

"And James would know that the food was delivered because he owns the damn company. He could have made the arrangements!" Addison cried. "Holy crap, Marian! You might be right." She looked at Rory, her eyes alight with excitement. "I think we just solved a murder mystery."

"Alright," Rory said, holding up his hands. "But before we go breathing any of this to the public," he eyed Addison sharply, "we need to check our facts."

"I know, I know, I know," she said excitedly. "I'm going to head over to the florist and get a copy of the receipt for those flowers. It's bound to have credit card information or a contact number or something."

Rory nodded and looked at me. "You need to keep researching our client list. Are you up for it?" I nodded and he offered me a hand, pulling me from my tangled sit.

"What are you going to do?" Addison asked him.

"I'm going to go back downstairs to the admin offices and keep an eye on our intern. If she tries to leave-" he picked up his gun off the desk. "I'm only half joking," he added dryly, moving towards the door.

Just about two hours later, I was printing off my findings. Of the hundreds of reviews we'd written over the last few years, 27 places were completely out of business with no rumblings of a second attempt. News articles had cited economic conditions, poor service and unfavorable reviews as reasons that many of the places had closed their doors. I took special stock of the ones that mentioned our personal reviews as having been detrimental to the business.

I was just starting to make copies when Addison barreled through my door with Rory hot on her heels. "Aren't you supposed to be watching Betsy?" I asked him, not looking up from the copy machine.

"She left to study for a test she has in the morning."

"There's not really a way to track if she's telling the truth without being creepy," Addison added.

"We could follow her." They both began to laugh as if this were perhaps the funniest thing they'd ever heard. Straight-faced, I continued to make my copies. "I was serious."

"Let's save drastic measures for drastic times," Rory said.

"That's not- never mind. Fine. Addison, what did you

find out for us?" She shot Rory a worried look. Something passed between the two of them that I couldn't quite catch and it made me anxious. They'd clearly already chatted through her findings. "Well?"

"Don't freak out," she said, gingerly taking a step towards me. "It might not be as bad as it looks."

"Well, how bad does it look?"

"Pretty bad," Rory said in a surprisingly upbeat tone. Addison shot him a look. "Well it does."

"Okay, look," I said, interrupting the spat. "My first love interest might have been hired to kill me. My intern might have been hired to kill me. The police department thinks I'm trying to kill myself as part of some big conspiracy. So please. Tell me. What could possibly be worse than all of that?" Addison handed me a copy of the receipt she'd gotten from the florist. "Well, there's nothing here," I said, handing it back to her with a shrug. "No credit card, no contact phone number. It's a dead end but it's really not so bad in comparison to the aforementioned issues."

"Well, it's not a total dead end," Addison said. "The person who ordered the flowers didn't want to do so over the phone because the florist would only take a credit card. Someone ordered in person with cash." She looked again to Rory. "The florist was able to give me a description."

"Well, that's an impressive memory. Does it sound like Betsy?"

Addie shook her head. "It was a man."

"James?" I guessed.

She shook her head again and handed me her notebook. I scanned the page, skipping over her questions and leads. Under House of Flowers she'd written an address, a phone number and – "Oh. My. God." I said, meeting her worried gaze.

"No wonder she remembered him, eh?" Rory said, attempting to get me to crack a smile. It wasn't going to happen. The florist had given Addie an exact description of Mika.

"What is happening to the world?" I asked angrily, thrusting Addison's notebook back to her.

"Should we call the police?" Rory asked.

I almost laughed but noticed he was serious. "No!" I admonished. "Last I heard from Barry, we were still suspects."

"You've worked with the police for years," Addie vented. "I just can't understand why when one of their own is in trouble, they point a finger."

"I'm not a cop," I said simply.

"Yeah, but you're still family. Extended, but that aside."

I shrugged. "I really wish I had answers. The only two that I ever got close to were Barry, who is doing what he can to help us from the inside, and Janet, who transferred out two years ago when her husband took up an assignment in Tampa."

"Do you still have Janet's number?" Addison asked. I could sense an idea forming in her head.

"I think so, we talk every once in a while," I said, pulling my phone from my pocket, beginning to skim through my list of contacts.

Addie nodded. "Call her. And call Barry. Ask them who else we can trust in the department. If we have to go with

171

the plan that Rory and I came up with last night, we're going to need a few allies." I nodded. "Then call Mika."

"What?" I asked, nearly dropping my phone. "Can you hear yourself talking?"

"Just ask him out for coffee," Addie soothed. "We need to see if we can find out more about why he ordered the flowers."

"Or if he's working alone," Rory added.

I paused. I hadn't considered that scenario. I'd simply been working under the impression that this was all James's doing. And until now, I'd never even considered that Mika, of all people, would be involved. So much for two incredibly attractive men being totally into me at the same time. What a joke. "It's probably better that I never became a detective," I muttered.

"You would make a brilliant detective," Addie said, coming to put her arm around me. "You're just emotionally involved all around here. Plus, it's technically your first case."

I gave her a small smile. "I've got some phone calls to make."

"Add James to your list of calls," she said, moving away.

"I have to meet with both of them?"

"I think it wouldn't hurt to let both of them think you're still into them despite recent events. If they are trying to kill you, especially if they're not working for themselves, a little human connection could go far in keeping you alive."

She had a point. An hour later, I'd left a message for

172

Janet, lined up a meeting with Barry on his day off that Thursday and set up coffee dates with James and Mika for that same evening. I could only hope that both men would let me live long enough that I'd still be around to hear from Janet and meet with Barry.

I was scheduled to meet with James soon. The coffee shop was just a short drive away. Rory was planning to drop me off and wait just around the corner in case an emergency escape was needed. "We're going to record this, right?" I asked as Addie was primping me with tools from her purse.

"Yes," she paused. "Oh, crap," she said, powdering my nose. "We can't, I gave the pin to Barry." She mused for a second. "That's okay, I'm sure we can figure something else out. We have..." she checked her watch, "30 minutes. Rory!" she barked.

He looked up from the computer. "Yes?"

"I need you to go to my office at the Journal. I have a tape recorder there. It should be somewhere in my desk. Can you make it there and back in less than 30?"

He stood and grinned. "At least give me a challenge." Pulling his keys from his pocket, he jogged for the exit. "I'll be back in a flash!"

Half an hour later, Addie had somehow turned me from frumpy to casual. She'd pinned my borrowed shirt so that it wasn't quite as busty in the front, smoothed back my hair, which had dried in a rather frizzy manner, and

173

glossed up my makeup with the products she kept in her purse. "You never know when you're going to have to coerce a Senator for comments," she told me as she glossed over my lips. Additionally, I had a small, handheld recorder taped tightly between my breasts. "We won't be able to hear what's going on but Rory will be just around the corner, watching the front door. I'm going to camp at the service entrance, just in case. Only dig if you feel comfortable. Otherwise, just work to establish the connection. You have about an hour before we have to take you to meet Mika," she told me.

Rory dropped me just around the corner from the coffee shop. Squaring my shoulders and taking a deep breath, I walked as confidently as I could to the entrance. I checked my reflection in the window, tugging slightly at my bangs so that they totally hid my gash. When I walked in, James stood and waved. He had scored us the comfortable, overstuffed chairs near the back by the fireplace. As I approached, I noticed that he seemed unsure of what to do with himself. That was a first. He finally settled for an awkward hug. "Sit," he told me. "What would you like to drink?"

Thoughts of a possible sense-altering drug being dumped into my coffee bid me pause. Still, this date wasn't about acting suspicious. It wasn't even about getting evidence. I had to appear trusting and unruffled. "Vanilla latte," I replied calmly, removing my jacket and flinging it over the back of a chair.

"Milk or soy?"

"Surprise me."

He smiled and strode towards the counter. I positioned myself in the chair closest to the fire with a clear view of James, the barista line and the counter where they placed finished orders. If anyone slipped anything into my drink, I would know about it.

The place wasn't very crowded and our drinks were ready shortly after James had ordered. I watched him pick up the two bright mugs of piping hot drinks and carry them over eagerly. There was no funny business. He handed me my latte with a bright smile and took the chair beside mine.

"I can't say I'm surprised that I had to be the one to reach out for date two," I said in a way that I hoped sounded flirtatious rather than annoyed.

He laughed nervously. "You were pretty upset the night I dropped you off," he said. "And then that thing with your car." He stirred at his drink distractedly. "I didn't think you'd ever want to see me again."

"You could have at least sent flowers," I chided. "You do seem to know where I work, after all."

"I-" he stopped, seeming to catch himself. Had he been about to tell me that he'd been behind the flowers that were sent to my office?

I looked at him curiously. He was clearly uncomfortable. I could see things taking a very different turn if I didn't steer the conversation another direction. "Anyway, I'm glad you agreed to meet with me!" I said brightly, totally changing the subject.

"You are?" he asked, surprised.

"Well, of course!" I continued. "It was so great seeing you the other night and I never had a chance to say thank you for dinner."

"But what about the other girl?" he asked, clearly confused. "I was just trying to make it look like old habits die hard. I wasn't actually interested. She was a little young for me. But I could tell all the way to dinner that you still saw me that way- like the guy who stole your virginity in the back of a beat-up car. But Marian, the only one I was interested in that night was you."

He looked so sincere that I had to fight my overwhelming urge to believe him in order to focus. "Oh, something about having a near-death experience just makes you forget silly things like that," I said, pulling my feet up into the chair, even as I shuddered internally with just how easy I must seem. "Let's just start over. Hi, I'm Marian," I said, holding out my hand for him to shake.

He smiled and took it, shaking firmly. "I'm James," he responded eagerly.

"So, tell me about yourself James."

For the next hour, we talked about everything except what we each did for a living. I didn't push him to share any details that he wasn't willing to disclose and by the time I stood to leave, just under an hour later, I was positive that on some level, I'd made him care about me. At

176

least a little bit. "Great catching up with you," I said, stretching. "I have to be off."

"Another hot date?" he asked teasingly.

"Who told you that you were hot?" I teased back.

He smiled. "Is it with that other guy?" he asked.

My smile froze. "What other guy?"

"The guy from your studio Friday night."

Adrenaline coursed through my veins as I struggled to find a response that didn't sound ridiculous. "Why would you care?" I finally stammered.

I saw a flash of something in his eyes, but then it was gone. "Have fun," he said. "Just be careful."

"Why would I need to-" but he gently brushed past me and made his way through the front door. The room suddenly felt very cold. I shivered involuntarily, despite the heat that prickled my skin from the roaring fireplace.

Collecting my coat and purse, I, too, made my way out the door and down the block, to where Rory was waiting, hunched down in his SUV. "Any idea where he was headed?" he asked as I slid into the front seat.

"Nope," I told him. "But close your eyes for a second." He complied and, as swiftly as possible, I tugged the recorder free and slid it out for inspection. "Okay, you can open them," I said as I pressed the pause and rewind button. "But listen to this." With that, I played back the last part of my conversation with James.

"What did he mean by that?" Rory asked.

I shrugged. Just then, Addie stumbled up to the window,

her face hidden beneath the hood of an enormous parka. "Anything good?" she asked eagerly. I rewound the tape and played the last part of the conversation for her. Her eyes brightened and she let out a low whistle. "We can use that."

"He could just be jealous," Rory suggested. "Telling Marian to be careful because Mika is a player."

Addie smiled at him, amused. "I like that you always see the potential best in people," she told him.

"Somebody has to in this relationship," he muttered, starting the car.

Addie handed me a fresh set of batteries through the open window. "Get that sucker back on," she said with a wink. Then she was gone, huddled in the wind, clacking her way back to her car on her red heels, made brighter against the muddied ice and snow that lined the sidewalk. She really was ridiculous. I loved her.

A few minutes later, we pulled just around the corner from where I was set to meet Mika. All patched up and ready to go, I smiled at Rory with a confidence I didn't actually have.

"Don't let what James said bother you too much," he told me, placing a hand over mine. "Addison and I are right outside if you need us. Besides, he's not going to try anything drastic in public."

I nodded and stepped from the car, striding towards the entrance. Mika was nowhere in sight. Checking my watch, I noted that I was a few minutes early. Again, the coffee shop was nearly empty and I had my pick of tables. As such, I decided to go ahead and order my own drink.

No sooner had I settled into a table with my mug, than Mika walked in the door. You know how in movies when someone really beautiful walks into a room, the whole present crowd just stops whatever they're doing to stare? That's pretty much what happened. The men eyed him enviously as the woman looked on, unashamed by their brashness. I could feel all eyes turn to me as he sat down at my table. Slowly conversations around us started up again, but the two of us sat there, looking at one another and not speaking for what seemed like hours. "I'm going to go grab a drink," he told me finally.

I nodded and looked about the room as I waited for him to return. He did, just moments later, with a steaming cup of plain black coffee. His eyes hadn't met with anyone but me his entire absence. I felt an inner glow, no matter how hard I tried to squash it. "No frills," I teased, nodding at his drink.

"I like to get to the point," he said, his eyes growing dark with interest as they scanned my neck and collarbone. I swallowed and nervously sipped my coffee. He leaned back in his chair and did the same. "I was planning on calling you tomorrow morning to ask you out for dinner tomorrow night."

"I guess I just didn't feel like waiting," I responded nervously.

"I liked it," he said. "I don't mind being old-fashioned, but

179

something about a woman taking control of a situation. Any situation. Is, well- hot," he said, blowing on his drink.

I was momentarily hypnotized by his lips. Through my daze, I somehow remembered the entire meaning of our meeting. It was possible he was working in cahoots with the killer. Heck, it was possible that he WAS the killer. I needed to make Mika see me as human, not as lunch. "Well I'm glad you see it that way," I said, taking back control of the conversation, shaking off my daydreams. "I had fun the other night. I'd be interested in learning more about you."

"And I you," he said with a grin.

Something in his smile sparked an angry fire inside of me. I hated myself for finding him so attractive. I hated myself more for the feelings I was trying to wrestle down. Unfortunately, they weren't simply lust-fueled. We'd had a real connection last night. Or at least, I had. Still, he was content to treat me like a business transaction and I was just going to have to figure out how to do the same. My life depended on it. I swallowed away the anger and gave him a small smile. "Well, let's get started."

The next hour zipped by. Even though I didn't have anywhere else I needed to be that evening, I imagined that Rory and Addie would be going out of their minds with worry if I didn't come out for air soon. And thus far, Mika had offered nothing to incriminate himself as the individual who had ordered the flowers. Still, I was out of time. I began to gather my things. "Leaving so soon?" he asked, surprised.

"Yeah," I responded, brushing my hair back behind my ear. "I've got an early day tomorrow at the studio. It has been kind of a long weekend. I should get some shut eye."

"Oh, okay," he said, standing too. He stepped around the table and picked up my coat, holding it open for me. Smiling, I slipped my arms into the sleeves and allowed him to come in closer than was necessary as he closed it tightly around me. I felt his hot breath on my ear and closed my eyes, hating myself for feeling turned on in that moment. Still, our conversation today had given away no hints that he was out to kill me. Everything had been curious and flirtatious. A real conversation. I was sickened by how easy it had come to us. And yet—

His breath was still hot against my ear. I could feel curious eyes taking us in. Clearly, I wasn't the only one feeling the searing heat between the two of us. It was evident to the entire room. Mika slowly brushed a lock of my hair forward and quickly, stealthily, gave my ear an almost indiscernible lick and bite. I gasped involuntarily and my eyes shot open.

I was in such a state that I almost didn't hear the words he whispered next. "Did you like your flowers, Marian?"

My mind went completely blank and I stood, frozen in fear. "Wh- what did you just say?" I asked, not flinching. "The flowers," he asked again. Was it my imagination, or had his voice suddenly taken on a dangerous, mocking tone? "I know I shouldn't say anything. It's rude to ask, but you haven't mentioned them."

I pulled myself away, tripping over my chair. People were staring. I was blind with terror, not caring what was going through their heads. I had to get out of there. I whirled around to stare down Mika, blinking back the tears that were stinging my eyes. How could I have been so stupid? I let my guard down for one second and he'd moved in for the kill. Clearly, the entire attraction was just in my head. I'd been dumb enough to believe that someone that looked like him could actually be attracted to me without some twisted end game in mind.

"Marian?" he asked, his eyes darkening with concern. "What's wrong?"

"What could you possibly mean?" I hissed quietly. He started to say something else but I cut him off. "Don't bother." With that, I turned and hurried out of the cafe with what little dignity I had left. Outside, I looked left and right, searching for Rory's car. It was snowing again and I squinted through the whiteness but didn't see him.

"Marian!" Mika shouted, stumbling out into the snow after me.

"Leave me alone!" I cried, clutching my purse and walking hurriedly towards the back of the building. Surely, Addie would be sitting back there, waiting.

"Marian! Stop! Please!"

The strain in his voice made me hesitate, but I didn't stop. "I know what you're trying to do," I called back to him. "And it isn't going to work. I'm not interested in your sick game of cat and mouse." There! I could see Addie's car, exhaust lazily rising from her tailpipe in the cold snow. Strengthened by just how close I was to escape, I whirled around to face Mika and drew myself up to look as large and angry as possible.

Mika paused. "Woah," he muttered, holding up his hands and taking a step back.

"I'm finished with your sick mind games. And James's too, if that's who you're working with."

"The guy from your studio?"

"Don't play stupid," I spat. "You just gave yourself away and there's no taking that back. Tell James that I'll be ready for him."

I heard a car door slam shut and turned to see Addison, bundled up in her parka, hands shoved deep into her pockets. "You okay?" she called, eyeing Mika suspiciously.

"Fine," I called back. Turning back to Mika, I leveled him with a stare. "Remember what I told you. Oh, and I never,

ever want to see you again." Spinning around quickly, I ran the last few steps to Addie's car. "Get in," I barked to her, opening the passenger door with a snap. Once we were both inside, I turned to look at her darkly. "Go." She shifted the car into gear and slowly we rolled past Mika, who was nothing more than a dark shadow against the heavy snow.

"What happened?" she asked me a few minutes later, once we were a safe distance from the coffee shop with no signs of a tail.

I was digging through my purse, looking for my cell. "First, I need to find Rory," I muttered. "I'll tell you both back at his apartment."

She nodded and aimed her car that direction.

When Rory frantically answered my call, I had half a mind to chew him out, but resisted. "Where were you?" I asked through gritted teeth.

"I'd been parked in that spot for an hour. Someone from the city knocked on my window. Said I had to move or I was going to get a ticket. I was just driving around the block! When I drove back by, you weren't inside. Are you okay?"

I sighed. It was impossible to stay mad at him for that one. "I'm fine," I murmured. "Addie and I are headed back towards your apartment. Can you meet us?"

"Yes, I'll see you there."

"Great," I said, clicking off. Leaning back into my seat, I felt my body go slack. Laying my head against the cool glass, I struggled to rein in my tears. I was sick of crying. I was sick of feeling helpless. I drew in a breath and focused on the angry fire that was nothing more than a dull ember in my stomach, trapped below the roaring flames of fear and uncertainty.

Addison and I arrived back at Rory's apartment first. When we got upstairs, she reached up to the light that was hanging just outside his door. After feeling around for a few seconds, she grasped a key and used it to unlock the front door. Replacing the key, she followed me inside. "I'm going to make us some tea," she told me, making a beeline for the kitchen.

Saying nothing, I made my way over to the reclining leather chair and all but collapsed into it, forcing it to rock violently back and forth for a few seconds. I couldn't be bothered to care. A few minutes later, the teapot was whistling away on the stove and the front door swung open to reveal a very panicked and disheveled looking Rory. When he saw that both Addison and I were safely inside the apartment, he relaxed considerably and began removing his gloves and jacket. Addison brought each of us a steaming mug of a very musky smelling substance before going back to some for herself. She and Rory each took a seat on one of the armrests of my chair. We all sat in silence for a few moments with only the occasional slurp to distract us from our thoughts. Finally, Addison broke the quiet. "Tell us what happened."

Not even caring about Rory's presence, I lifted my shirt

186

and gently removed the recorder, which was still taped between my breasts. Gentleman that he is, he blushed slightly and turned away. I hit the rewind button and waited for a few seconds before hitting play. However, the last piece of conversation that was crystal clear was just before Mika helped me into my coat. His menacing inquiry about the flowers was completely indiscernible. "Damn it!" I screamed, lifting my arm to fling the recorder across the room.

"Don't!" Addison cried, catching my hand mid-hurl, wrenching the recorder from my grasp. "That still has everything from your meeting with James on it. Just tell us what happened."

I took a sip from my tea, drew a shaky breath and filled them in. When I finished, I took another sip of tea and waited for their reactions. Suffice to say there wasn't much. They were both stunned into relative silence. Eventually, Rory cleared his throat. "So we know that on some level, he's involved."

"It sure does seem that way," I answered.

"What was he saying to you when you were walking towards me?" Addison asked, curiously.

"He was confused about why I was upset. Acted like he had no idea what his connection might be to James."

"So just playing head games," she surmised. "Unless they're not working together at all."

"Unfortunate," Rory piped in.

We stayed just as we were, sipping our tea and not

speaking for a very long time. Finally, I looked to Addison. "I need to go home."

"You can't go back there," she told me alarmed. "It was obvious that whoever broke in last night had been interrupted. What if they come back?"

I shrugged "I'll deal with that if it happens. Fred needs food." I stood and went to place my empty mug in the sink. "And frankly, I could use some fresh underwear and a pair of my own clothes."

"I'll stay with you then," Addie said, coming to stand next to me as I gathered my things.

"Addison, I don't need a babysitter." I reached into my handbag and pulled out the fuzzy sock I'd stored in there, shaking the gun free from it and into my hand. "Besides, I have a gun." It was a lot larger and heavier than I remembered.

"Jesus!" Rory cried, nearly dropping his mug. "How long have you been carting that beast around in your purse?"

"Just since yesterday," I told him. "After it turned out that Alec was murdered, people kept encouraging me to buy a gun. So I did." I tucked it back into its sock and slid it into the front pocket of my purse.

Addie eyeballed the pocket suspiciously. "Any idea how to shoot that thing?" she asked.

"Not exactly."

"I need a vodka," Rory told us tiredly as he stood and walked to the kitchen.

"Not so fast!" Addison told him. "You need to come with

us to check out Marian's apartment."

"That gun is going to blow a hole the size of London into anything that so much as looks at you." Rory said. "Which is more than I can say for what I'd be capable of."

"Please?" I asked pleadingly. "I know I come off as tough and controlled, but there's just nothing quite like a strapping young gentleman such as yourself to check things out for me."

Rory rolled his eyes. "Bullocks. Fine."

I've never been afraid to go home before. Take it from me, it's not a great feeling. Home is supposed to be where you feel safe. The one place that makes sense when everything is falling apart. Where the heart is and all that crap. While I still saw it as my haven, I also had to admit that being away had enhanced my fear of returning. Still, when we finally stepped inside, I felt an overwhelming sense of peace. "There's no one here," I said, turning to Rory and Addison.

"I haven't even checked out the scene. How do you know?" Rory asked.

"I just know," I told him. "You guys can go home."

"Don't be ridiculous," Addison said before Rory could walk out the door. "We're going to stay with you for a little bit. Make sure you don't need anything."

"No, really," I promised. "I just would like some time alone."

"If you're sure," she told me.

"Yes."

"Very well then," Rory told us, stepping over and handing me the keys to his SUV. "We will just take Addison's car back to my place."

"You sure?" I asked.

"Yes," he answered. "In fact, why don't you keep it? I've been meaning to get something more updated."

"Oh, Rory. I couldn't!"

"No, honestly. You need it."

"You forget he's loaded, Marian. Take it," Addison supplied.

"And the truth about why she finally came around to me is out," Rory smiled as he put his arms around Addie, giving her a quick kiss on the cheek. "Frankly, I'm glad she said it because if I were to say it, I'd sound like an arse."

I smiled. "I think the thing that I love about you the most is that I do forget that about you. Often," I said, clutching my hand around his keys. "Well, thank you. Really."

"My pleasure. Take good care of the magic school bus."

"Magic?" I asked, curiously.

"Please don't ask him to explain," Addison told me, shoving Rory out the door. "It's more information than you need about our relationship."

Wrinkling my nose, I shut the door behind them in mock disgust. Turning, I laid my head against it and sighed, looking around. "Well, Fred, time to get this place cleaned up a bit."

The next morning, I awoke to a loud, obnoxious banging against my front door. By the time I'd gotten everything set to rights in the apartment from the break-in, it had been well into Monday morning. I'd stumbled into bed just as the sun was beginning to peek over the eastern horizon and had pulled my curtains tight, intent on sleeping in. Clearly the universe had other plans in mind. "Marian!" Addie said, pounding hard, again. "Marian open up! This is important."

"Mmmpf," I muttered, tossing a pillow into the hallway and rolling over, tucking myself deeper into the sheets.

"I know you're in there!" she cried, banging again. "The bus is still parked right where Rory left it."

Damn. Sighing, I pulled myself out of bed and lazily made my way over to the door. With a large yawn, I opened it and peered blurry-eyed into a huge bouquet of exquisite mixed flowers. Cautiously, I began searching for a card. "Who are they from?" I mumbled.

"Good morning to you, Sunshine. Or rather, good afternoon. These were delivered to the studio over lunch."

"I'm surprised they didn't blow up your trunk," I muttered, searching harder through the stems.

"Looking for this?" Addison asked dryly, pulling a small

191

red envelope from her pants pocket. I snatched it away from her and realized it had already been opened. "Well, you can't really blame me. And anyway, Rory did it. I was at the Journal this morning and swung by the studio to take him to lunch. The flowers had just been delivered. He was curious." She paused, waiting for my reaction.

"Who are they from?" I asked again, eyeing her suspiciously. When she just stared back, I ripped the card from its envelope and began to read. "Thanks for dinner Saturday night. Hope to see you again soon. Mika." My eyes widened and I met Addie's gaze. "Oh, no. He probably thinks I'm a total nut job."

"Probably," Addison said, thrusting the flowers into my hands. "At least you didn't threaten him with the gun."

"He clearly meant for me to get these yesterday," I mumbled, walking them into the kitchen, arranging the vase prettily by a window.

"Obviously," she answered, flopping down on the couch. "As for why they didn't make it, who knows? Either way, you should probably try giving him a call." She reached for my house phone and held it out to me. "Sooner rather than later is best in this case. Trust me."

Hesitantly, I took the phone from her hand. "I will. Just not right now. Let's get our heads wrapped around this first."

"What do you need to wrap your head around?" she asked me. "Adonis sent you flowers. He's not our killer and he thinks you're cray-cray. Call him. Now."

"Well, hold up a second!" I cried. "If he didn't send the other flowers, then who did?"

She shrugged. "I have no idea. James, probably."

"We're missing something. Something big," I told her. "You're the journalist, for crying out loud. You're supposed to sniff out the stuff no one wants to tell you. It's how you make your living."

"You're the crime scene photographer," she shot back. "If anyone should have a clue, it's you. Everything is in the details, Moyer. We'll figure it out. In the meantime, call him. Please. For me. If this one goes to waste, I will never forgive you."

Glaring, I went to retrieve my cell from the bedroom and flipped through my recent dials for his number. I waited anxiously while it rang. Once. Twice. Three times. Four. Voicemail. I let out the breath I'd been holding and waited for the beep. "Hey, Mika. It's Marian. Look, um, I think I owe you an apology. I got your flowers. Today. They uh-well, I mistook another delivery for yours the other day." Addison shot me a look and made a "wrap it up" motion with her finger. "Anyway, I'd like to see you again so that I can explain. Give me a call." After I rattled off my number, I hastily hung up the phone and dropped it onto the couch like a hot potato.

"That was…intelligent," Addison said.

"Shut up, you're the writer."

"Call Barry. Find out if they have anything on the fingerprints from your break-in, yet."

"You're bossy today." I called his desk phone and he picked up halfway through the third ring. "Nothing yet," he told me. "But I promise to let you know as soon as I find out."

"Think Addison could get it out of someone?"

"Possibly, but probably better not to try," he said. "Don't want anyone to know you're sniffing around. Hey, you care to fill me in on your suspects?"

"I wish I had more to tell you," I groaned. "One of our leads just fell through. We're back to square one."

"Still thinking it could have been that James guy?"

"Pretty sure. But he had to have had some help."

"What makes you say that?"

"Can we talk about this Thursday? Addison and I have a lot work to do between now and then."

"Oh, sure, sure. I'll see you then."

"Great," I said, hanging up. Turning to Addison, I asked, "Anyone else?"

"No word from Janet?"

I shook my head. "She must be really busy. Sometimes it takes her a day or two if she's knee-deep in a case."

"Fair. Have you had lunch?" My stomach growled and she smiled. "Guess that answers that. Take a shower- let's grab sushi, I'm starving."

"I'd really like to just go back to bed."

"Shower. Sushi. Not up for debate."

"Didn't you have lunch with Rory?"

"No, I decided it would be much more fun to play your

errand girl."

"Fine," I grumbled, making my way to the bathroom.

An hour later, I was clean, dressed and aiming the bus towards *Sushirama*. "I feel like I'm going to run somebody over in this thing," I said to Addie as I turned onto a side road.

"You probably could," she answered. "But it would probably work in our favor right now if you didn't."

Once we were seated and done checking over the menus, I folded my hands and leaned across the table. "What's our next move?"

"I'm afraid that we may have to resort to the original plan," she said.

"Well, do what you have to do."

"When do you meet Barry? Thursday?"

"Yeah, why?"

"The plan requires getting tough with the police. I don't want him to be around to take the heat that's bound to follow."

"Awful sweet of you."

"I have my moments." She sipped at her cucumber water and turned to look out the window at the passing cars. "I still can't figure out who broke into your apartment. Or why. What could they possibly be looking for?"

"Maybe whoever it was, was really just looking to freak me out," I said. "It's part of the game."

"Perhaps," she said, cupping her chin in her hands. She tilted her head slightly as if she'd heard something. "Is your phone ringing?"

I started to dig through my purse and pulled out my cell. My eyes widened as I viewed the display. "Mika," I mouthed.

She gave me the thumbs up. "Go talk. I'll get our order in."

"I should probably wait until-"

She snatched the phone out of my hand and hit the answer key. "Marian's phone," she answered in a singsong voice. I shot her a dirty look. "No, but she's right here, Mika, hold on just a moment."

She held the phone out to me but I shook my head. Standing, she leaned across the table and shoved the phone up to my ear. "Mika!" I said, refraining from kicking Addison's chair as I stood and hurried towards the quiet hallway near the restrooms. "I didn't think you'd ever call me back."

"Your message sounded sincere enough," he answered. "A little crazy, but definitely sincere."

I let out a laugh that sounded more like a honk. Clearing my throat, I ignored the fear that was bubbling in my gut and rushed forward. "Well, I really just wanted to say that I was sorry, even though I'd rather apologize in person, but I wasn't sure if you would see me. Anyway, there was a big mix-up with the flowers."

"Seems that way."

"Well, I- I- um."

"Listen, don't take this the wrong way, but it just seems

196

like you could use someone to talk to. Are you free later?"

"Tonight? Yeah. Yes. I mean, I can be."

"Great. 7 o'clock. Same place as yesterday."

"Swell," I said under my breath, but he'd already hung up the phone.

As I made my way back to our table, Addison looked up. When she saw me, her face grew pinched with worry. "Did he not want to hear it?" she asked.

"Oh, no. He wants to hear it. All of it," I said, sipping my water quietly. "I'm meeting him tonight at the coffee shop again."

"Same one as yesterday?"

"Yup."

"That's evil. And somehow pure genius. I like it."

"He apparently likes things to be even."

"Can't be all bad," she said with a wicked smile. "Who knows where else he's going to ensure that everything is even?"

I threw my napkin at her and laughed. "I haven't even begged for forgiveness yet. Let's not hurry up to the part where we have sex."

"Oh, beg for forgiveness," she said dirtily.

"Addison!" I scoffed. "We're in public."

She giggled. "What time do I need to have you home to get ready?"

"We have most of the afternoon."

"Perfect. Then after this we're going shopping. My treat. You need something fabulous."

After a stop through the local mall and trying on about 30 different outfits, I finally settled on a soft, caramel brown scoop-necked sweater and a pair of gold hoops. "Add a pair of jeans and your knee-high brown leather boots and he'll practically be apologizing to you," Addison promised as she handed me the bag the cashier had just handed her. "Let's get you home."

After a long, lingering hot bath filled with lavender sea salts and quite a few bubbles, I hurried to get ready. The final outcome wasn't nearly as stunning as the magic that Addison had been able to work on me for my previous dates with Mika, but it would do in a pinch. Giving my hair one last fluff in the mirror, I grabbed my keys to the bus off the kitchen counter and locked up. Taking the stairs two at a time, I almost plowed into my neighbor, Mr. Hanley.

Mr. Hanley is 73 years old, totally deaf in his left ear and somewhat blind. He walks using a gold cane. It looks like something he stole off of a pimp in the seventies. Granted if you ever met the man, you'd probably assume he used to be a pimp in the '70s. Something in his eyes. Why he still takes the stairs up nine floors is beyond me. "Sorry!" I said, jumping around him and zipping on down the stairs.

"Careful!" he cried, clutching the rail and shaking his cane my direction. "I'm crippled."

I pulled into the parking lot of the coffee shop right on time. Sending Addison a quick text to let her know that I was still safe, I leapt out of the bus, slammed the door and hurried towards the front of the coffee shop, trying hard not to slip in the well-packed snow. This time, when I walked in, Mika was already waiting at the same table as yesterday. I smiled, shook my head and walked over. "You sure do enjoy punishment," I said, taking a seat and removing my coat.

"Oh, you have no idea," he answered with a wicked smile. "Vanilla latte?" He pushed the warm mug towards me and I gratefully picked it up, drawing in a long, delicious sip.

"You remembered," I told him.

"Oh, I remember quite a few things from last night."

Embarrassed, I looked down at my lap as I pulled off my gloves and dropped them into my purse. "I'm really sorry about that," I mumbled.

"You're what?" he asked playfully, leaning towards me.

I laughed. "Sorry. I'm. Sorry."

"Tell me what happened."

"It's just really complicated." I eyed him shyly. "You don't really strike me as the complicated type."

"Try me."

With a heavy sigh, I recounted the past few weeks from start to finish. Alec's death. The autopsy results — both fake and real. The trip to see my parents. The date with James that seemed incredibly suspect. The fact that he was likely working with an accomplice. The fact that I was still considered a suspect by the police. The fact that I'd considered Mika a suspect. The exploding car. The ransacked apartment. The threatening flowers. That what he'd said the night before had set me off.

When I finished, I took another long sip of my latte and waited, not looking at Mika. Recounting all of it was exhausting. There was no way he wouldn't run screaming in the other direction. Not now.

"Marian?" he asked gently. I tapped my fingers against the table and tried hard to steel myself against what I was bound to see when I finally decided to look at him. Swallowing back the tears that were welling up, I lifted my gaze and was met with genuine concern. "I probably would have freaked out, too," he said with a small smile.

I laughed and swiped at the tears that had gathered in the corners of my eyes. "I'm so sorry," I told him. "It's just the way everything kind of added up."

"You really don't have to apologize any more," he told me, taking my hand in his. It was warm and smooth. Darker than my own. Heavier. I immediately felt relaxed.

We sat for the next while in silence, sipping our drinks and holding hands. When our mugs were empty, Mika picked them up and placed them in the busser bin up by the front counter. "Ready?" he asked when he returned, holding out his hand. I took it and stood. He reached around me and picked up my coat, holding it open like he had the night before. This time when I slipped into it, he made no advances.

I'll admit that I was slightly disappointed as I pulled my gloves from my handbag. As we walked towards the exit,

Mika stepped in front of me to hold open the door. I thanked him and stepped through it, into the frigid night air. "Well," I said, hugging myself, trying hard to ward off the cold. His hands were stuffed deep into his pockets. Our eyes met. "Thanks for coffee and for the talk and-"

Without warning, he stepped forward, took my face in his hands and kissed me. I felt my knees beginning to weaken and he snaked one arm down around my waist to prop me up while the other moved slowly to the back of my neck and then to my hair, where he gently tugged my head back. I gasped as he moved his lips to the exposed flesh on my throat, my limbs lax in his strong grip. My skin felt as if it were on fire. I could barely breathe. "Mika," I whispered.

"Let me come home with you."

I froze. Surely my ears were deceiving me. "What?"

"Just to be there," he said. "Just to take care of you."

"Oh. Sure." I licked my lips.

He laughed, mistaking my idiocy for sarcasm and tucked a wayfaring curl behind my ear. "Honest," he promised, pressing his forehead to mine. "No funny business. But I haven't felt this way about someone in longer than I care to remember. I'd just like to make sure you're safe."

"I can take care of myself."

"Marian? Shut up and let me sleep on your couch." With a chuckle I pulled away and began walking towards the bus. "I'll follow you there," he called after me.

While I'd like to be able to confess that there was funny business — and quite a bit of it — Mika was true to his word and slept peacefully on the couch the entire night. When I awoke the next morning, he had replaced the couch pillows, folded the blanket and was sipping quietly on a cup of coffee as he flipped through an old edition of *Food Porn*. When he heard me shuffling out of the bedroom, he looked up and smiled. "Morning. I hope you don't mind that I made a pot of coffee. I just wanted to see you. Find out if you needed anything before I left."

"Just coffee," I muttered.

He laughed. "Not a morning person?"

I shook my head. "Best not to start leading you on now." I stopped, realizing what I'd said. "I mean…assuming that this, er, that we, ah, that this continues."

"Touché." He finished the rest of his mug in one quick swig and stood. "I'll let you do your thing. If you need me, you have my number." I nodded and yawned, pulling a mug from the cabinet. In a flash, he'd rounded the counter, flipped me around and planted a kiss right on my lips. "Bye," he whispered, pulling away.

Just like that, he was gone. All I could do was blow into my cupped palm and sniff, hoping that my hasty tooth brushing before entering the kitchen had been enough.

Later that day, I sat curled in one of Addison's chairs in her office at the Journal. "He just...slept?" she asked, appalled. "On the couch?"

"Yeah," I said, bewildered. "I mean, he said that he was going to, but I didn't really believe him."

"And yet, you let him follow you home anyway," she chided.

"Maybe he's just not all that into me."

"He said he had feelings for you."

"Maybe he was just hoping to get into my pants."

"But he didn't try," she said, pausing to peer at me over her reading glasses. "He just said it. And then never touched you. It's like he's serious." We both thought about this for a few moments and then Addie went back to typing up her article. "I don't know," she said between clicks. "It sounds like there might be some actual potential. Which you deserve after multiple disappointments and your disturbingly long dry spell."

"Why don't you ever have dry spells?" I asked glumly.

"Because I'm not picky," she said without breaking her typing.

"But you still ended up with a winner."

"After a lot more bullshit. I'd prefer to have started dating Rory about three years ago rather than going through my endless string of fun losers."

"It's not like he wasn't interested."

"Sometimes, you just can't see it until you need to."

I squinted hard at her screen. "What are you writing?" I asked her, struggling to read the small type.

"Nothing," she answered, turning the screen so that I no longer had a view. "Or at least nothing that I can tell you about just yet."

"Is it all part of your big secret plan?"

"Yup."

"Looks like an editorial."

"Stop thinking about it."

I sighed. "Well, I'm going to head out. I just wanted to fill you in on my bizarre morning."

"Bizarre indeed," she replied. "Let's keep in touch this week. Let me know when you hear back from Janet. You feeling okay? Need a watch dog? I can call Rory."

"No, it's fine," I said, waving her off. "I'm headed over to the offices anyway. There's nothing to do at the apartment other than sit around and stare at Fred. Besides, Rory is piecing together the new issue. We send to print on Friday. I want to see Mika's spread." Addison's lips curled into an evil grin. "Don't," I warned her.

"What did I say?" she asked innocently.

No sooner had I walked in the door of the studio than my phone begin to ring. Smiling, I pulled off my mitten and grabbed the phone out of my pocket. It wasn't Mika. It was Janet. "Hey!" I answered in happy surprise.

"Hi!" she returned. "How in the heck are you?"

"I'm good, I'm good," I said, slowly pulling off my other mitten and my hat as I made my way upstairs to the office. "Glad you were able to call."

"The hubs and I were on a belated anniversary trip down south," she said lazily. "Ever been to Costa Rica?"

"Oh sure. I haven't," I laughed.

"You really need to go," she told me. "The beaches, the hiking, the mountains." She sighed. "I'm ready to go back."

"How soon until Rob retires?"

"You kidding?" she scoffed. "Even when he retires, he'll never actually retire. Not to the point where we could run off and live in another country half the year, anyway."

"Yeah, but you're in Florida, now. Life sure could be a lot rougher."

She giggled. "Very true. I'll count my blessings instead of continuing to whine. How much snow have you gotten so far?"

"About eight inches."

"We have a spare room. Right now, the dog is the only one who uses it."

"I may just take you up on that if things keep going the way they are," I told her.

"Your message sounded a bit worrisome. Care to fill me in?" I did. I recounted everything from start to finish, including Mika's sleepover and the editorial that Addison wouldn't let me see. Janet let out a low whistle. "That doesn't sound like the department I left behind at all."

"I know," I told her. "I'm so confused. And disappointed.

But I knew that I can count on you and Barry to maybe guide me towards a few more people in there who I can trust to give me the honest scoop."

"Barry Delcore?" she asked.

"Yeah."

"Huh. I didn't think he'd actually stay with the department. What's he up to these days? Was he promoted or anything?"

"He's a detective now," I said. "One of the younger ones. What made you think he wouldn't stay with the department?"

"You know he took acting in college, right?"

"Yeah, we went to both high school and college together," I told her. "But after his freshman year at the university, his dad said he'd only pay tuition if Barry took on a more serious career. He bounced around for a couple of months but one night during a study session I asked him to quiz me for a criminal justice class. He was hooked."

"Huh. That I did not know," she answered. "He just never seemed overly involved in the work. Changed partners a lot more often than the rest of us, too. Any idea who he's with now?"

"Carly something or another. I've only met her once."

"Carly Ipson," Janet supplied. "She was good people. Why don't you try reaching out to her? Frankly, I've known her far better and longer than I have Barry. But I guess you've known him a long time. Plus, I don't really like any men outside of my husband. And even he's questionable at times."

We both laughed and chatted for a few more minutes about work, men and the craziness that was life. After we hung up, I took a deep breath and let it out. I felt more at peace than I had in a very long time, as I always did after speaking with Janet. She was one of those people that you wouldn't speak to for a year but could pick things up right where you'd left off. Though she was a few years older than me, we'd taken to each other right away. She was like a big sister without all of the fighting and chaos.

Checking my watch, I decided it would be a fine time to pop in on Rory and convince him to take me to lunch. Downstairs, he was bent over his computer, fervently alternating between clicks and typing. "How's it going?" I asked him.

"Oh, fine," he said. "Almost done actually. And Mika is looking pretty good." He turned his screen so that I'd have a better view and I literally gasped out loud. "I know, right?" Rory said, turning the screen back so that he could focus on the typed review that was off to the left of the photograph.

"Photoshop?" I asked him, trying to peer around his head to take in the photo again.

"Nada," Rory answered. "You took some pretty inspired shots." I gently socked his shoulder. "Well, you did," he murmured under his breath. Click. Click. Click.

"Can you still make your deadline if you take me to lunch?" I asked.

"Sure can. And I'm driving." He clicked the save button and closed out of his computer. Standing, he grabbed his jacket off of the coat rack in his cubicle.

"You bought something new?" I asked, walking towards the exit.

"Didn't you see Addison earlier?" he asked. I nodded my head and pushed the back door open, the wind hitting my face sharply. At least it had stopped snowing for the time being. "I can't believe she didn't spill the beans," he said, pulling a clicker out of his coat pocket.

A gorgeous, silver car flashed its lights and beeped at us. "Is that an Audi?"

"Sure is," he told me, tossing me the key. "And on second thought, why don't you drive it?"

I hesitated, taking in the sleek curve of the car including the "In Transit" stickers that showed none other than today's date. The shiny silver hubcaps and the graceful lines of the bumper. "I don't think I should," I said, weakly holding out the keys to him, but he was zipping past me and sliding into the passenger seat before I could say much else. Gulping, I opened the driver side door and slipped behind the wheel. Hesitantly, I started the engine and felt the car let out a low, throaty purr. I laid my hands softly on the wheel and closed my eyes, feeling its power. "Time to let loose and do a little living, kid," Rory said. "Put her in gear and take me somewhere good."

Twenty minutes later, we'd pulled into the lot of our favorite dingy bar, Al's Burgers. Not only did they have an eye-popping array of beers on tap, they also served the best Juicy Lucy's in the city. As a matter of fact, Addison herself had written just that in her review of them about two years ago. Theirs had been one of my favorite photo shoots from over the years — with our entire gang, Rory and Addison included, posing with a Juicy Lucy and a pint of beer.

The studio had been filled with laughter that day. The models had been the only ones stripped down to their usual 'attire' but somehow, Rory and Addison had come into their own throughout the session. The final result was magical. I smiled at the poster-sized photo that Al himself had bought from us and enlarged. It hung behind the bar, above all the taps, for everyone to see. Next to it, in a much smaller frame, was the photo and accompanying review from *Food Porn*. It added some character to the dark bar, which was scattered with buzzy fluorescent lighting and cheap, standing room only tables.

Rory and I took two of the coveted stools that were situated along the actual bar. Al greeted us with a friendly wave and signaled that he'd be down in just a minute. He was in the process of drying pint glasses.

After lunch, I drove Rory back to the office. "You coming in or...?"

"I think I'm just going to head home," I told him.

"You sure? Do you want me to go with you?"

I smiled and handed him his keys. "No, I'm okay. Really."

He shook his head. "Of course you are. I just-" he paused and we looked at each other for a few moments. I reached out and covered his hand with one of mine.

"I know," I told him gently. "But I can't keep wondering if and when."

He covered my hand with his free one. "Good point."

I covered his hand with my free one and we played that game for a few seconds before I laughed and gave up. As we stepped out of the car, he grinned at me over the roof. "I'll email you the final mockup tonight," he told me. "Will you have time to do the sweep?"

"I'll be waiting," I grinned. "And based off of what I've already seen, I can't wait."

On my way home that afternoon, I turned up the radio and sang along with every tune I knew. I switched up the radio stations every once in awhile and bounced back and forth between mainstream pop, '80s and '90s music and an R&B station. The snow had started up again, but was only lightly dusting the roadways. The wind wasn't blowing at all.

I pulled safely into the parking lot of my apartment building. Checking around, I grabbed my purse and made a mad dash for the inside before anyone could pop out of the bushes and drag me away. As soon as the elevators dinged open on my floor, my phone began its familiar ring. I patted both coat pockets before starting to dig frantically through my purse. I finally found it in a side pocket. I'm not entirely sure why I never put it in the same place. It would make my life so much easier. "Hello?" I asked hurriedly, not bothering to check the number.

"Just hearing you answer the phone makes me smile," Mika told me.

I smiled, stopping in front of my door as I dug for my keys. "Is that so?"

"It is. What are you up to?"

"Oh, just got home. Went to go check out next month's issue. I'll get the rough draft from Rory tonight and it's set to go to print this Friday. There's this really hot guy featured. I kind of want to ogle the photos before anyone else can."

"Any chance I could get a preview?" he teased.

"I might know someone," I teased back, unlocking my front door. As soon as I stepped inside, the hairs on the back of my neck stood on end. "Wait a second," I said quietly, pausing in the hallway.

"Marian? What's wrong?" Mika asked, his tone slightly panicked.

"Someone was here," I answered. "I'll call you back."

"No. Marian, wait-"

I hung up and stuffed my phone deep into my purse and then set my purse on the floor near the door. Locking the door behind me, I removed my coat, knelt down and started rifling through my purse for the sock that held my gun. I wasn't totally sure how to use it, but it couldn't be that difficult, right? It was already loaded, after all. At least, I was pretty sure it was.

My phone started to ring again but I ignored it. Pulling out the gun, I slowly raised it, like I'd seen in every crime movie and television show I'd ever watched. The phone stopped ringing and the apartment plunged into silence. Seconds later, it rang again. Ignoring it, I peeked around the corner of the entryway and into the living room. No one was there. Slowly, I made my way around to the other side of the couch and gently pulled aside the curtains with the barrel of the gun. They were empty, too.

Spinning, I crept slowly into the kitchen. Opening my cabinets one by one, and finally the pantry door, I realized that it was all clear. Making my way to the opposite end of the apartment, I quickly checked the bathroom. Nothing had been disturbed. That only left one room. With a deep, calming breath, I tried to relax my shoulders. That's what they always said when characters were being taught how to shoot on television, right? Then, I tiptoed the rest of the way down the hall and gently pushed my bedroom door open with the barrel of my gun. I checked the closet, under the bed and behind the door. Realizing that everything was clear, I lowered my weapon and slumped to the floor. As I went to slide the gun onto my bedside table, I paused. The top drawer was slightly ajar.

As just about anyone close to me can tell you, I am obsessive compulsive when it comes to keeping things tidy. Dishes don't stay in the sink. Rugs remain perfectly straight. My drawers are always completely closed. It's weird, but it's my thing. I had not left that bedside table drawer open.

Timidly, I worked the drawer open with the barrel of my gun. There, sitting tidily in the middle of my clean, folded sheets was a cupcake swathed in a trademark *Yummy Tummy* wrapper.

I'm not sure how long I sat there. My phone had rung a few more times, but I continued to ignore it. I couldn't move. I couldn't think. I couldn't seem to remove my gaze from that stupid cupcake wrapped within the signature *Yummy Tummy* wrapper.

"Marian?" asked a voice from the doorway. Screaming, I stood and reached for the gun. "Woah, woah, woah!" Mika said, raising his hands. "It's okay, it's just me." Shaking, I slowly lowered the gun. He approached me with caution, his hands still raised to show me that we wasn't hiding anything. "You didn't pick up. I got worried."

Something occurred to me and I quickly raised the gun again. Mika paused. "How did you get in?" I asked, my voice deathly low.

He hesitated. "Your door was unlocked."

I shook my head and kept the gun level at his chest. "It wasn't. I locked it when I came in. After I hung up with you."

"You didn't," he said, taking a tiny step forward.

I got the feeling that he was sizing me up, trying to figure out how he could wrangle the gun out of my hands. "Stop!" I cried. He did. "Quit talking to me like I'm crazy. I'm not crazy. I know I locked that door."

"Put down the gun and let me explain."

"No."

"Marian. Please."

"There's a cupcake in my drawer. Did you put it there?"

"A what?"

I motioned to the drawer with my head. "Come look," I told him. "Slowly."

He looked befuddled, but did as I asked. "Why did you put that there?" he asked me.

"I didn't!" I shrieked. "Someone has been in my apartment. Someone put that there. Now tell me, how did you get in?"

"Okay," he said, slowly reaching out. "I'm going to take the gun and we're going to talk about this. Look at me. Look at me, Marian." I did. I searched his eyes completely. "Give me the gun, please." Slowly, keeping my gaze locked with his, I handed him the gun. He looked visibly relieved. After a few quick-handed movements, he was peering into the bullet chamber. "This isn't even loaded."

"Oh," I said, sitting back down on the bed.

"Do you even know how to shoot this?" he asked me, incredulously.

"Maybe I just wanted you to think I had a loaded gun," I said matter-of-factly.

"You never unlocked the safety."

"The what?"

"Oh, Marian. I'm going to teach you so many things."

I felt a stirring in my nether regions, but fought hard to

ignore it. "How did you get in?" I asked him again.

"I'll get to that," he promised. "But first I need you to tell me what happened."

A bit later, we were sitting at the kitchen table. Mika had made himself at home, boiling water for tea and setting out two mugs. "You can't stay here by yourself tonight," he told me. "It's dangerous."

"I'm tired of staying with other people," I told him. "I'm not leaving. James has already been here. He's probably not going to come back."

"Why are you so sure that it's James?" he asked.

"The cupcake was clearly from *Yummy Tummy*," I answered defensively. "And it's obvious that he is involved in some shady business. He told me himself at dinner."

"First of all, anyone could have simply bought that cupcake," he told me, handing me a mug filled with steaming hot tea. "Second of all, what is this obsession with James?"

"It is not an obsession," I scoffed. "I've just known him a long time. We have…we have history. And now he's trying to kill me."

"If he is trying to kill you," Mika said, taking a seat backward on a chair, "then it sounds like it's just business." I glared at him and contemplated dumping my tea on his head. "What kind of history?"

I froze. "I don't want to talk about it."

"Well, if it's history, it shouldn't matter. Spill."

I cleared my throat. "We dated. Well, date. We went on a date. Once."

"Go on."

"And then we…well, we slept together. Later. Another time. A long time after our date." I tugged at my sweater. It was getting incredibly hot and uncomfortable in the kitchen. "I kind of- he kind of- was. Well, the first. One. And then…well, it was just once."

"Ah."

"But that's all over now. I mean, I'm not interested in him like that anymore. He's trying to kill me, after all."

At that moment, my phone started ringing in my purse in the hallway. "I'll get it!" I cried, jumping up and almost running out of the kitchen. By the time I got to it, it had stopped ringing. Just as I swiped the screen to see who the missed call was from, it started to ring again. James.

"Are you going to answer it?" Mika asked amusedly as I stood stock-still by the couch. I shook my head. Mika stood and strode over to look at the ID. "Well, you have to get that," he said, tugging the phone out of my hands. "You think he's trying to kill you, you have to make plans. Lure him into a trap and all that. Hello?" he said, answering for me.

My eyes grew wide with fear and I struggled to grab the phone, but Mika held me off as he listened to James speak on the other end of the line. I couldn't tell what was being said, but Mika's grin continued to grow wider and wider. "Hold on, just a second," he said into the phone. "Let me get her for you."

With a wink, he handed me my cell and waltzed back into the kitchen, whistling. I couldn't believe I hadn't shot the bastard when I had the chance. "James!" I said with false enthusiasm. "Sorry about that, my brother just doesn't- I mean, he-. Um. How are you?"

"I didn't know you had a brother," James said cooly.

I prickled. "There are a lot of things you don't know." Pausing, I took a breath and put a happy tone back into my voice. "Did you need something?"

"Yeah," he said. "I was really glad you called the other day. I wanted to take you out for dinner, again. Date three, but we'll pretend it's only date two."

"Oh," I said, unsure of how to respond.

"Is your- is your brother taking you out this week?" Did I denote a hint of jealousy in his tone as he spoke? "I didn't realize you had a sibling that hailed from the Ukraine."

"I- wait, how did you know that his accent was Ukrainian?"

"Uh- someone I worked with had a similar accent," he stammered. Clearing his throat, he added, "But anyway, what night are you free this week?"

I wasn't sure what to do. On the one hand, it would be easy enough to set him up. On the other hand, he clearly had a wider skill set than I did. Who knew what plans he'd carry out while we waited to meet? Better to make it as soon as possible. But not too soon — I didn't want to appear overly eager. "How's Thursday?" I asked him.

By Thursday night, I'd have caught up with Barry, as well as Addison and Rory. Chances were that Addison's plan would have already been carried out by then if she was working on it earlier today. The police department would be on our side after that. It was the perfect cover.

"Thursday is great," he answered. Begrudgingly he added, "Tell your brother that James said hello," and then he hung up.

"Bye," I said to no one. Lowering the phone I stared at it for a moment then looked up at Mika. "He said to tell you 'hello.'"

"Very sweet of him," Mika said. "How about you and I plan a date this Friday to celebrate your capture of a killer?" he chuckled and took a sip of his tea. Standing from his chair once again, he walked by and gave me a quick kiss on the cheek. "I'll be back tonight."

"Where are you going?"

"I have to run an errand," he answered. Grabbing his coat from the rack in the hallway, he shrugged it on and opened the door. Turning to smile at me, he said, "Don't forget to lock this."

"Doesn't seem to keep you out," I muttered. "And you never did tell me how you got in."

Mika shrugged sheepishly. "Nasty habit I picked up as a kid."

Later that evening, I was curled up in my fluffiest pajamas, skimming through the latest rough draft edition of *Food*

Porn on my computer. Rory had really outdone himself
with the layout, which was a toned down throwback to our
early days. It was the perfect, subtle "Happy Birthday" to
the magazine. And Mika. Wow. It should have been near
impossible to forget what lay underneath all of his jeans
and plain, faded t-shirts, but somehow, I hadn't quite
remembered it like this. I ran my finger over his abs that
filled nearly my entire screen. Okay, so I'd zoomed in a
little. Looking down at my own slightly rounded belly, and
then examining the Reese's I held poised in my hand, I
suddenly felt self-conscious. What could he possibly see in
me?

There was a gentle knock on the front door and I quickly
stuffed the Reese's in my mouth and set the laptop next to
Fred's tank. Tiptoeing towards the door, I paused to peer
through the peephole. It was Mika. Once the door was
open, I gave him a small smile. "Surprised you didn't just
let yourself in," I teased.

"I only do that in the case of an emergency," he answered
easily, pulling off his coat and hanging it next to mine. He
scanned me up and down. "Ready for bed?" he asked. "It's
only 8:30."

"Just looking at the draft Rory sent over earlier for our
next edition," I said, walking over to the computer and
sitting back on the couch.

"Oh, can I see?"

"I didn't take you as the vain type," I teased, handing him
my laptop.

He blushed. "I hope I'm not coming off that way. I guess I just don't see myself the way so many other people seem to. I'm hoping to maybe get the answers from your magazine." He slid through the pages, swiping at the screen to bring up each new one. When he reached the end, he handed the laptop back to me and shrugged. "I still don't get it."

I smiled and closed it down, then set it next to the couch. "Want a glass of wine?"

"Sounds wonderful. In fact-" he stood and walked over to his coat. Reaching into a side pocket, he pulled out a tall bottle. "I picked some up on the way."

He handed it to me and I read the label as I walked to the kitchen. "Sounds fancy."

Mika shrugged. "Clerk recommended it. I honestly don't know all that much about wine."

"Me neither," I confessed, pulling a bottle opener from the drawer. "I tend to just grab something cheap from the bottom shelf and call it good."

He laughed at this. I turned to grab two glasses out of the cabinet. Setting them on the counter, I began the process of uncorking the wine. In the middle of my effort, Mika fit himself perfectly up against my back and wrapped an arm around my waist. With the other, he gently pulled my loose curls back and softly, gently kissed the nape of my neck. I felt my entire body shudder and I almost dropped the bottle of wine. Setting it back on the counter, I turned. His eyes had grown dark, as stormy as a troubled sea. I felt his arm that was around my waist tighten. He free hand gently caressed my face. Suddenly, his lips were on mine. They were warm. Soft. Inviting. They parted and our tongues touched playfully. One of us moaned, but I wasn't sure whom, nor did I care.

Both of his hands slid slowly, gently, to the backs of my thighs. Then he was lifting me up, setting me on the kitchen counter. My fingers were running wildly through his hair, the back of my head pressed hard against the cabinets. My eyes were closed in absolute ecstasy as he purposefully, methodically began to unbutton my top. I wasn't wearing a bra, so that removed a significantly awkward step. This was going to be amazing. And anyway, what were we on here, really? Fourth date? Fifth? That was acceptable timing, wasn't it? Hopefully he didn't think that I was a total — gasp! His fingers were pushing hard against that spot. His lips were kissing my chest, prying at the remaining buttons with his teeth.

My home phone started ringing and he paused. I clutched his head between my hands, holding his face to where he was poised, just at the small rise of flesh that was my heaving bosom. "Don't. Stop." I said through gritted teeth.

"What if it's one of your friends?" he asked, his voice buried in my chest.

I sighed and hit my head hard against the cabinet. "Damn it," I muttered. Struggling to button up my top, I flopped off the counter and hurried over to the phone.

Scanning the caller ID quickly, I groaned. "It's my mother."

Mika smiled and picked up the bottle of wine that hadn't quite been uncorked. "You should answer," he told me. "They're probably just worried about you."

Sighing heavily, I answered with a grumbly "hello?"

"Well, thank goodness. I haven't heard from you in days. I thought you could be dead. Don!" she screamed. "Don, she's alive."

"I told you she was fine," I heard my father grousing in the background.

"Oh, who asked you?"

"You did. You said, 'Don, do you think Marian is okay? We haven't heard from her in days.'"

"Well, I just-"

"Ma!" I said, cutting them off. "I'm fine. Really."

"Well, how's the case? Can you update us on the case? Your dad stopped trying to call after Barry wasn't able to get anyone to connect with him. Hoped that would make a difference for you."

"Now really isn't a good time," I told her.

"Well when would be a good time? You're always so busy." I could imagine her leaning hard against the kitchen counter, one hand feistily placed on her hip.

"Saturday," I promised her. "I'll even come out for a visit."

She gasped. "Don, she said she's going to come visit us! Saturday!"

"I'll bring Addie," I promised. "Gotta go, love you." I made a quick kiss noise and hung up the phone.

When I turned around, Mika stood smiling in the kitchen, holding two glasses of red wine. "Close to your parents?" he asked.

"Kind of," I answered. "I mean, we used to be. But then when I started the magazine, things got a little rocky. We still love each other, I mean, I'd do just about anything for them. My brother and his family, too. But we were never the type to sit down and have dinner every Sunday, you know?"

He nodded. "I do."

We made our way over to the couch. He sat on one end, while I sat far away on the other. We sipped at our wine, talked about our families and laughed the entire night. Eventually, when we came to a comfortable lull in conversation, Mika smiled at me and took my wine glass. Setting both his and mine on the floor, he gently pulled me over to his lap and we laid down on the couch together. No words. Just holding. Granted, I'm pretty sure that, that wasn't a gun in his front pocket, unless it was an unusually large, pointy gun.

When I awoke in the morning, I found myself alone on the couch. Rising slowly, I glanced around the apartment, but it was empty. I listened quietly for noises down the hall, but there were none. I was alone. Puzzled, I stretched and stood. As I made my way into the kitchen, I found a note taped to the coffee pot.

Had to meet a client. Call you later. PS: You're quite the snuggler when you're asleep.

Quite the snuggler? I wasn't entirely sure what that meant, but I had a feeling it would be embarrassing. Best to not ask any follow-up questions.

After making a pot of coffee and munching on a bowl of cereal, I retrieved the wine glasses from last night and tidied up the kitchen. With my second mug of coffee in hand, I retrieved my cell from its spot on the counter, where it had remained unplugged the night before. I flipped briefly through my missed calls and texts. When nothing overly important popped up on the *Food Porn* front, I decided it was a safe bet that I could work from home. I retrieved my laptop and took up my position on the couch, curling my legs beneath me and balancing my computer on my knees. As it fired up, I took a sip of coffee and gazed out my windows. The sun was reflecting brightly off of the snow. I squinted, looking carefully out towards the city skyline.

Wednesday flew by. I'd stayed perched on the couch nearly all day, making general edits and notes for Rory. By the time I sent everything back to him, it was well into the afternoon. I called Addison to check in and tell her about the cupcake debacle. Needless to say that she was thrilled when Mika had once again proven himself to be a knight in shining armor. While we spoke, I briefly pondered retrieving the creepy cupcake that was still sitting atop my neatly folded sheets but decided against it. It might be needed later for evidence. Plus, I had much more important matters from last night to focus upon.

"Why didn't he make another move?" I moaned.

"Why didn't you?" she challenged.

"I haven't known him that long."

"If he's going to break your heart, he's going to break your heart. There's no way to avoid that. Do what you feel," she told me. "Look, I have to go. We'll chat tomorrow."

Something about the way she said "tomorrow" made me recall that Thursday was D-Day. Barry would be out of the office and Addison would be carrying out her evil plot. Whatever it was.

Next, I left a message for Carly Ipson, as Janet had suggested. From the sound of her voicemail, she was out until next week. While I couldn't necessarily wait that long to gain favor this time around among the department, I figured it couldn't hurt to start building up for future usage. I left a cheerful message asking her to meet me for coffee when she was back in the office.

Mika called, as promised, to check in. Before we said goodbye, he asked, "Are you sure you're going to be okay tonight?"

I smiled into the phone. "Yes. The creepy occurrences usually skip a day. I think I'm safe for today."

"I'll be working most of tomorrow," he told me. "But call if you need anything. Especially tomorrow night."

"I'd like to come see your workshop," I told him. When I was met with silence, I quickly added, "But if that's weird or it's too soon, that's totally fine."

"No, it's not that. Um-" he paused. "We'll make arrangements for that. Maybe Friday after dinner."

"Unless I'm dead," I muttered.

He chuckled. "I have no doubt that if anyone is meant to survive the circumstances, it's you."

After we hung up, I spent the rest of the day alternating between napping, eating and watching Johnny Depp movies. I contemplated yoga — I hadn't been since all of this craziness began weeks ago. But somehow, I couldn't bring myself to drag all of my issues into an environment of zen. It just didn't seem fair to the others that would be in class.

Somehow, I managed to get up off the couch and into my bed that night. My dreams had been fitful, to say the least, and I awoke Thursday morning feeling anxious. I had no idea what Addison's plan was that day, which made everything so much worse. How can you prepare for the fallout when you don't even know what to prepare for?

I wasn't meeting Barry until noon and it was still early morning. I allowed myself to linger in the shower until the water grew cold. Once I'd gotten myself ready for the day, there was nothing to do but wait. If I went to the office, I'd probably drive Rory to the brink of insanity with my nervousness. I was far too jittery to drive, anyway. So I forced myself to relax, making breakfast tea instead of coffee. I did, however, allow myself the indulgence of Christian Bale's company in the background, though I wasn't really paying much attention.

The home phone rang about an hour into my movie. On a Thursday morning, it was likely a telemarketer. I let it ring. It stopped, but immediately started back up again. "For goodness sakes," I muttered, walking over to scan the caller ID. I didn't recognize the number, but it was a local area code. Seeing as how I didn't have any creditors after me at the moment, and considering the magnitude of my day that lay ahead, I decided it was in my best interest to answer. "Hello?"

"Marian, it's James."

I felt my blood run cold. "How did you get this number? It's unlisted."

"There are other ways," he said mysteriously.

I gulped. "What do you want?"

"Just wanted to call and check in. Make sure we were still on for tonight. Is your- your brother still there?"

"No, he left," I said, taking momentary satisfaction in his jealous tone. He totally knew that Mika wasn't my brother. "And I'm still up for tonight if you are."

"Great. Should I pick you up at your apartment? Say around six?"

"Sure. Whatever. You remember where I live." It wasn't a question.

"Not sure of the apartment number."

"I'm sure you'll figure it out," I said coolly, hanging up the phone. I realized that I was shaking, my veins pulsing with adrenaline. I wasn't looking forward to that night at all. Silently, I hoped that all would go according to plan, that Addison's plot, whatever it was, would make the department see reason. That Barry would have a few more insights to offer when we met. That I would still be alive come the midnight hour.

A short time later, my cell began to ring. Picking it up, I noted that it was Barry and groaned aloud. He only ever called on a day when we were meeting because he was running late. "I'm running late," he told me. "I have a few errands that I need to get to. Can we meet this afternoon instead? Maybe two?"

"That's fine," I told him. "Just text me where I should meet you."

"Roger that," he said, and the line went dead.

Sighing, I shuffled over to the couch. I once again

debated leaving the apartment but decided that, for now, it was better to stay put. No use putting myself in harm's way when things appeared safe and sound right here at home.

I'm not entirely sure what time I fell asleep. I awoke with a start, a movie preview with a lot of guns going off blasting through my dreams. I checked the clock on the wall. 1:30pm. I'd need to meet Barry soon. However, when I looked through my missed texts, he hadn't sent me a place to meet yet. I sent him a brief message. A few seconds later, my phone began to ring. "Hey, Barry, I was just wondering-"

"Marian?" said a voice on the other end of the line. It wasn't Barry's.

"Yes?" I asked, momentarily confused. "Who is this?" The voice sounded achingly familiar and yet, I wasn't able to figure out whose it could be.

"It's Lynette. From the precinct."

I nearly dropped the phone. "Hey, Lynette. It's been a few weeks."

"I know," she answered. "Hey, I know it's a bit of short notice, but I was wondering if you were free to take some photographs."

"Photographs?"

"For a crime scene. Over on Wisconsin Avenue."

"A crime scene?" Boy, did I sound intelligent.

There was a pause. "Is this Marian Moyer?"

"Yeah, Lynette, it's me. I just- I haven't heard from anyone over there in weeks. With everything going on, the case and stuff, I'm just surprised to hear from you. Who asked for me?"

"The Captain," she answered. "Said whoever they've been using is still too green. But for whatever reason, no one had been able to get in touch with you for a few days. As it turns out, your number was wrong in the system. I figured that one out," she added proudly.

"Lynette, my number has been the same one that has been in the system for years."

I could see her shrugging. "Don't ask me. All I need to know is if you're free to take a few photos this afternoon or if you've got other plans."

"I'm free," I told her, still in a semi state of shock. Barry would have to wait. And I needed to call Addison and tell her to hold off. "I can be there in 30 minutes."

Lynette rattled off the address. I thanked her and hung up. Next, I tried calling Addison, but received no answer. I contemplated leaving her a message, but it seemed too complicated. I hoped it wasn't too late to stop her plan, whatever it was.

Call me. Important. The text to her sent, I checked again for a message from Barry. There were none. I sent him another follow-up.

Clearly the whole incident with the police had been a mix-up. I briefly wondered how my number had gotten mixed up in the system, but didn't allow myself to question

233

it too long. I needed to get ready.

I sent Barry another brief text that said I needed to postpone our meeting, but that we absolutely needed to still touch base that day. Gathering my cameras, I allowed myself a quick touch-up in the bathroom mirror before hurrying towards the door. I dropped my gear so that I could put on my coat, hat and mittens. Finding my car keys at the bottom of my purse, I slung everything back over my shoulder and opened the door.

As I turned to lock up, I caught movement out of the left corner of my vision. Looking up, I was surprised to see none other than Barry. "Hey!" I said. "I just texted you. I can't meet up right now, after all. The department just called and-"

Slowly, he pulled an incredibly large, cold-looking revolver from his coat pocket. "Get back inside, Marian."

I was completely frozen. Have you ever had a gun pointed at you? I hadn't. For the record, you pretty much want to pee your pants. At least, that was my initial reaction. Fear was followed by shock. "Barry?" I asked, unable to compute why he was pointing a gun at me.

He motioned the gun towards the door. "In. Now."

Now I was starting to get pissed off. I don't take kindly to orders. Unless those orders include "take off your pants." I turned to face him and raised my gaze to meet his. "No."

"Excuse me?" he asked, narrowing his eyes. "I'm pretty sure I have the gun, here."

"What are you going to do, Barry? Shoot me in the middle of the hallway?"

"If I have to." His eyes grew even colder. Something told me that he wasn't kidding. I stood there for another beat, weighing my options. Sure, I could tear down the hallway, screaming at the top of my lungs. However, with the exception of crotchety, deaf old Mr. Hanley, my neighbors were mostly young working professionals with day jobs. I had no doubt that Barry's gun, unlike my own, was fully loaded. I imagined myself being shot in the back, writhing on the floor of my apartment complex while he walked away. I'd be discovered, stone-cold dead in a few hours. The building had no security cameras. I'd just be one more dead body in a string of *Food Porn* related murders. A second option was to unlock my door and try to dart inside without being followed, but that didn't seem very likely seeing as how, again, he was holding a gun. He'd probably just shoot his way through. The third option was to just do what he said and pray that somehow, someone would come save me. While I wasn't a huge fan of the damsel in distress motif, I didn't see much other choice that resulted in my remaining alive. With an angry huff, I turned and unlocked the door. "Atta girl," he whispered, menacingly.

"Shut up," I muttered. As soon as I went to push the door open, Barry shoved me inside and followed quickly behind. For a moment, my mind went to the gun stashed in my purse and I went to dig. I panicked when my hand couldn't seem to find it. Suddenly, I remembered. It was in my bedroom, put back into my dresser after the whole misunderstanding with Mika.

He seemed to sense my frustration. "Are you missing something?"

"Nope."

"Where's your gun?"

Damn it. I refused to answer or make eye contact. I tried to think quickly, but my mind was a jumbled mess of fear and anger. I had to focus.

"Where?!" Barry screamed, jabbing the gun into my chest.

"It's at work," I lied, easily.

He studied me for a moment. "You'd better be telling the truth." Motioning towards the couch, he added "go sit down." My phone's chipper ringtone began to sound. I desperately wanted to answer with something as natural as a bloodcurdling scream, but decided to wait for instruction. When I got to the couch, I turned around and sat down, placing my purse at my feet. Barry stood by the coffee table, his gun leveled at my head. "Kick your purse over here," he told me. When I did, he began rifling through it, throwing things on the ground as he went. My wallet. A coupon. My notebook. A tampon. "Jesus," he muttered angrily. "How do you even find anything in here?" The phone had stopped ringing by that point. When he finally found it, he checked the screen for the missed caller. "Addison," he scoffed. "Bet she's calling to tell you there was a little mix-up over at the police station."

His evil smile took on a slightly unhinged quality. Without warning, he threw my cell phone to the ground and stomped on it with his oversized, steel-toed boots. "Hey!" I cried angrily. "What the hell did you go and do that for?" He shrugged, but continued to smile and point his gun at me. Now I was less afraid and a lot more pissed off.

Just then, my house phone began to ring. The two of us stared at it until it flipped over to the message machine. My pleasant greeting ran and then clicked over for the caller to leave their message. "It's Addison, I need you to pick up the phone." There was a short pause. "Please, Marian, this is really important." Another short pause. "Well, I just tried your cell again and from the sound of things, you've turned it off. Call me, Marian. As soon as you get this. It's about Barry. We have to talk before the two of you meet." She paused again and sighed. "Please."

I continued to stare at my one remaining outlet to the outside world and prayed that Barry wouldn't smash it, too. Thankfully, he was far too distracted by his own genius to do any further damage for the time being. "I can't believe you didn't figure this out sooner, Marian," he said, gleefully. "You were so convinced that it was James!"

Okay, he had me there. The more excited he got, the more he was flinging around the gun. It was making me nervous. I had to keep him focused until I could figure out a plan. "Why did you do it? Why did you kill Alec?" I asked.

He scoffed at this. "I wasn't trying to kill Alec, stupid. He just got in the way. You want to know what they found in his system in addition to poison? THC. A lot of it. As fate would have it, he got the munchies and decided to break into the studio the night before the photo shoot, knowing full well that *Yummy Tummy* would have already delivered the goods."

"Did you poison all of it? Every single thing they delivered?" I asked incredulously. That would have been a lot of work. Not to mention a huge risk.

"Just the cupcakes," he answered. Then, with a wink, he

added, "You never could turn down sweets, could you?"

Again, he had me there. Distractedly, I rubbed my belly, which rolled just slightly over the waist of my pants. Barry looked momentarily disgusted by my soft gut, but then began to dig deep into his coat pockets. Finally, he retrieved something small and silver. He threw it to me and I fumbled briefly, but caught it. It was the pin I'd been wearing on my date with James.

"You'll recall that Addison gave it to me. The night your car exploded. Said that there was a recording of your entire date with James. I knew someone had to have a copy."

As discreetly as possible, I pushed the tiny pin-sized button on the back. It probably wouldn't connect to anything, but it sure was worth a shot. "You're the one who broke into my apartment," I said, taken aback. "That's why you were in the neighborhood! That's why you responded first to the break-in call!"

"Amazing how easy it is for you to put the puzzle together now that you're not filled with a sense of revenge for your playboy lover."

"But- my car exploded, first. James picked me up at the studio instead of meeting me!"

"That was just a big old coincidence," Barry laughed, but then his face grew dark. "I should have anticipated a remote starter in Wisconsin."

"The flowers!" I cried. "Why didn't the florist remember you?"

"I hired an errand boy. Already had the card written and sealed. Paid cash. Addressed it to the magazine, not you specifically. The fact that Mika went in to purchase flowers for you a day later, again, was pure coincidence. Can you blame their front office for not remembering some pimply teenager on an errand, but being able to give you an ab-by-ab description of a model? That model?"

My head was spinning. I was glad to already be sitting down. If I wasn't, I think that I may have fallen over.

"You broke in again. The other day."

"I just wanted to ruffle your feathers a bit. Things were getting a little too intense. It's important to have a little fun too, right?"

"You're sick."

"Maybe a little. You know, I think the best part was just how much you wanted to believe me. Every word I said, you lapped it up like a stupid dog. I convinced you that the department was out to get you. I inverted your phone number in the calling tree so you wouldn't be asked to photograph and you'd feel like the kid who got sent to the corner. The night your car exploded and Addison told me about the recording of your date, I knew that if I could just find that damn audio recording, I could frame James and be the hero of the hour. It would have been almost more enjoyable to kill you at that point," he added. "After you testified against him. Put him away for life. Then I kill you. And you carry that guilt with you to your grave knowing that you're the only one who can exonerate him."

I prayed that the pin was somehow recording all of this. If I didn't make it out of here, I at least wanted my friends to be able to prove that Barry belonged in the loony bin. "Who were you trying to kill, exactly?" I asked. "I mean, I realize that I'm clearly a target. But I don't really understand why. Were you after anyone else?"

"Of course not," he answered. "That's your problem, Marian. You never bother to try to understand anyone but yourself and your little circle."

"You were in my circle!" I shouted. I was livid — totally and completely beside myself with anger towards this man that I'd treated as a friend.

"Then how did you not know that I moonlight as a pastry chef?"

The last pieces were falling into place. I felt like I'd been slapped. "A chef? You mean, you work with *Yummy Tummy*. That's how you managed to poison our order. You were the last one to see it before it was delivered," I gasped. "You're the one who ordered the exclusive with us!"

He shrugged again and smiled. "James and his partner came into a lot of money when they were private investigators. Frankly, I don't think he had a partner. No one has ever seen the guy."

"James is a PI?"

Barry seemed delighted by my complete naivety. "He used to be. As in, he's not anymore. Solved a case one time down in Tennessee. A big one. Moved back here after that

241

to avoid the notoriety. He and his supposed partner freelanced for the MPD when the department was overloaded, but they didn't want to be looked to as saviors. The department managed to keep their names out of the press. Then came retirement."

"That's why Addison never picked up on it. James essentially doesn't exist for the police. Even his payroll, whenever it existed, was probably under a fake name."

"Thank God your degree wasn't a total waste," Barry muttered. "It was so expensive. Anyway, James and his fake partner invested in a few startups, including a dot com company and became billionaires. One of the startups was mine, of course. *Yummy Tummy, Inc.*"

"But no paperwork refers to you as the CEO. Anywhere. No reviews mention you. You're a ghost."

"Exactly. The whole business was set up."

"Just for this?"

"Just for this."

"That's a lot of hatred, Barry. You ever think about talking to a therapist?"

A vein in Barry's neck bulged and his face went red with anger. "Shut up!" He screamed, waving the gun in my face. I felt myself shrink back into the couch, my eyes wide with fear.

I was quiet for a long while after that. When I finally spoke, I was thoughtful. "I still don't understand why you're trying to kill me, though. You moonlight as a pastry chef. You own your own pastry shop. We've never

242

reviewed you, until this month, and believe me, the reviews are glowing. Why all the hatred?"

"You probably didn't even taste anything," he said sadly. "Not after Alec's untimely demise."

"But you'd never know it from the reviews!" I said, very chipper. "So…why do you want me dead?"

He laughed bitterly. "Is it really so difficult for you to guess? Think, Marian. Think really hard."

I thought. I thought as hard as I possibly could, given that I had a gun aimed at me. Still, nothing popped immediately to the surface. I shrugged helplessly.

"What did I want to be? More than anything else. All through high school. All through college."

"To act?" I asked.

"You mean to model," he told me. "Acting was a means to modeling," he sighed and wagged the gun at me again. "Don't you ever pay attention to anything?"

"I guess not. But in my defense I was pretty absorbed in a few things. Starting a publication that I wanted to be nationally known, for one."

He snorted. "You ruined my dream because you were selfish. How original."

"What are you talking about?"

"Every. Single. Modeling call!" he screamed. I shrank back into the couch again as he glared, pacing back and forth. I prayed that I would become invisible. It wasn't working. "I came to every. Single. Modeling call you've ever had," he howled. "And I've never once made it through the doors before you found your guy."

"Wait a second," I said, growing irritated again. I was back to being pissed off. "You wanted to kill me because I wasn't your gravy train? I worked my ass off to get to where I am."

"I was your friend," he cried. "You should have wanted to help me."

"You should have just asked!"

Barry laughed bitterly. "Oh, is that all I had to do?"

"Probably not all, but it would have been a great start."

"Really?"

"Yeah."

"I suppose it's too late for that now."

"If you let me go, I'll see what I can do," I pled, trying hard to keep my voice level.

He laughed again. This time, there was no feeling behind it whatsoever. My body grew cold. That probably wasn't good. "I can't do that, Marian."

"Well, why not?"

"You expect me to believe that we're just going to forget about this? That no one else knows I'm here?"

"No one does!" I said. "Who else could possibly know?"

He was contemplative. "I guess that, that's true." He paused. "But Addison has probably pieced it together. I didn't leave much of a trail, but now that she suspects, it won't be hard to fit the pieces together. What do we do about that, Marian?"

Just then, there was a knock on the door. "Marian, it's

244

Richard."

Barry glowered and turned to look at the door before whirling back towards me. "Richard?" he mouthed.

"Richard?" I asked loudly.

"Yes. From the other night. With Addison. The van," he said through the door.

"Oh, no," I whispered quietly. It seemed as though activating the pin had made me live somewhere out in the world after all. Now what was I going to do?

Being live right now was incredibly unfortunate. It's not like I would have let Barry off scot-free. Still, I didn't need to let him know that until I'd busted free. Something told me I'd been close to leniency — possibly even escaping without so much as a bleeding wound. Now, though. Now, I was probably screwed.

"What do you want?" Barry asked him loudly. He kept pointing the gun at my forehead, but occasionally began to slide it towards the door, just in case someone decided to break through.

"Hey, Barry. I'm Richard."

"I don't care if you're the pope. What the hell do you want?" Barry asked again, leveling the gun at my head once and for all, staring at the door.

"I want you to tell me what it is you want, Barry," Richard said kindly. I'd never seen the man, but I imagined he looked a bit like a soft, old grandpa. I was sure he'd be the kind of grandpa that bounces his grandkids on his knee while reading them books. I liked Richard. I really wanted to meet him. That probably couldn't happen if I were dead. I had to think of something while I still had brains to think.

"I want to be famous!" Barry shouted at the door, deranged. "And Marian could have launched my career!"

247

"You've had other dreams come true," I said desperately. As subtly as possible, I pinned the small, silver ribbon to my shirt. I wanted every single word to be crystal clear for the recorder, not muffled by my fingers.

"What? Baking?!" He threw his head back and laughed long and low and hard. "I told you, that was a cover."

"Pretty elaborate cover," Richard called through the door. "Surely you had to get some satisfaction out of your job."

There was a long pause. "I guess I didn't hate it," Barry muttered.

"And you worked your way up to detective. That had to be a proud moment," Richard added. "You've had a lot of successes, Barry."

Barry's chest puffed out with pride. "That's true."

"So why blemish your record?" Richard asked. "You don't want to kill Marian."

I felt my heart swell with love for Richard. Of course Barry didn't want to kill me. Richard knew it. I knew it. Barry knew it too; he just needed some guidance through the whole mess. I silently prayed he'd allow Richard to be the voice of reason.

"Don't I?" Barry asked, cutting his gaze from the door, to me, and back to the door. "I mean, what a way to get famous. Think of the headlines."

"Hey, Barry!" It was Addison, also on the other side of the door. How long had she stood there, listening to this maniac talk? I also noted that she seemed unusually chipper considering the circumstances. "Listen," she went

248

on. "It sounds like there was a bit of a misunderstanding. But I work for *Food Porn*, too, remember? Marian and I would be happy to have you come in for a photo shoot for our next edition."

Barry looked at me and narrowed his eyes. "What's the catch?"

"No catch!" Addison called. "We just need you to open the door. Let Marian out. Get rid of the whole hostage situation thing."

"I can't do that," he called, stepping closer to me, the gun still aimed at my forehead. I silently cursed my mother's genes for my unusually large forehead and wished that Barry would point the gun elsewhere. Then again, why would he? The only target larger than my forehead was my butt, and I was sitting on that. "How do I know you're not lying?" he asked her.

"You have to trust me," Addison responded.

"I don't trust any of you," Barry muttered quietly under his breath.

"Why?" she called.

His head snapped towards the door. "How did you hear that?"

"Uh…"

Barry turned back towards me and raised his gun again. "Answer me!" he screamed, just as his eyes locked onto the pin. His eyes widened and his mouth formed into a perfect "O." Slowly, he stepped closer and closer until he was inches from my bosom, which was heaving with both fear

and loathing, all generated by the man in front of me.
Putting his mouth right up to the pin he said, "Of course."
He waved the gun in front of the pin. Violently, he reached
forward and ripped it from my shirt, dropped it to the floor
and crushed it under his heel. In the process of removing
the pin, he also managed to rip part of my top away,
revealing my brand new purple push-up bra. I was going
to wear it to seduce James into a confession. Of course,
now I could just use it to seduce him. Assuming I got out of
here alive. I mentally slapped myself for thinking about
sex. "Nice bra," Barry told me. "Dr. Vick's?"

"What gave it away?"

"I bought one that looked similar for an ex a few months
ago from the place."

"Oh. That was nice of you."

"Barry!" Addison hollered. "Are you listening to me?"

Barry took a few steps closer to the door, but kept the
gun trained on me. I tried leaning a bit to the left, then a bit
to the right, but he kept adjusting his aim. "What did you
say?" he asked her.

"I told you that I can make you famous. I can
sensationalize your story for the Journal. You know I
write for them. You've seen my stories. I'm good. Really,
really good. I can tell people about how smart you are.
About how you fooled all of us. Even the police."

Barry's eyes suddenly lit up. I could practically see the
Hollywood stars spinning about inside of them. He
lowered the gun and moved to open the door. At that

moment, the window to my right exploded. I screamed and covered my ears, dropping from the couch to the floor. My front door flew open in a smattering of wood splintering and locks breaking. Somewhere, in the middle of it all, Barry was on his knees, howling in pain, clawing at the arm that was attached to the hand that was no longer holding a gun.

Suddenly, Mika was inside, pointing a handgun at Barry's head. He kicked the gun that Barry had dropped across the length of the room and was telling him to put his hands on his head and to not move. Within seconds, my apartment filled with cops. They flooded into my living room, filtering into my kitchen and down the hallway to my bedroom, like ants covering an apple slice that a child dropped to the ground. It all happened so fast that I didn't even realize that James, Rory and Addison were kneeling next to me. A gruff, older looking man who resembled a very stern Santa Claus was cuffing Barry. He looked just as I'd imagined, that old gruff Richard from Chicago. Perhaps a bit younger than I'd expected, but really, quite spot on. Then Mika was hauling Barry to his feet and handing him off to a police officer dressed in uniform.

"Are you okay?" Addison was asking me at an abnormally loud volume. She gripped my arm tightly and then shook me hard when I didn't immediately respond. "Marian? Marian!"

I blinked. I couldn't stop staring at the bizarre scene that was playing out in front of me. Barry was screaming for medical attention as the cop shoved him towards the door. "Police brutality!" Barry cried as he was recited his Miranda Rights. His angry face twisted as he turned to look at me one last time before he disappeared around the corner. "I'll get you for this," he swore with a growl.

Just then, Mr. Hanley peeked around the corner. "I can hear you loud and clear!" he complained. "Doesn't even help much when I turn down the hearing aid. All this violence is shaking the whole building. Shame on you! Shame." He turned and tottered back to his apartment next door.

Someone draped a blanket around my shoulders as someone else started firing questions off to me.

"Not right now," Mika said, walking over and pushing the questioning offender aside. "Give her a few minutes."

Two hours later, I sat on my couch, holding my third steaming mug of hot tea. James and Mika sat on either side, while Addison and Rory cooed over my empty mug and my blankets that apparently needed near constant fluffing.

As it turned out, Barry was one of the very few people in the police department who knew James as a private investigator. It was more due to the circumstances of their supposed friendship than anything else. Turns out that Barry had vented his frustration and even hatched his plan for the perfect murder in James's presence, then laughed it off as a joke before requesting the money to back *Yummy*

Tummy, Inc. James decided he'd do everything exactly as Barry requested, including leaving Barry's name out of all the owner paperwork. That way, Barry's fragile mental state didn't break at a point where James didn't have any proof beyond the crazy ramblings of someone who was clearly psychotic. He could keep an eye on Barry. He could also keep an eye on me — whom he admitted to developing quite a crush on over the years.

What James hadn't counted on was me spotting him outside my apartment that day. He'd been doing a routine check on me. The same routine check he'd been doing every week since *Yummy Tummy* first opened its doors just about two months ago. He knew that once the business was officially in full swing, it was only a matter of time before Barry would set up the photo shoot. Barry, however, had been quite smart even going so far as to set up his plans from a throwaway phone so that the poisoned goodies couldn't be tracked back to him. Still, when James found out that Alec was dead, he knew things were in motion that he couldn't control from the outside. He needed someone that had an excuse to sniff around the studio. That individual came in the form of Mika, James's former partner at the PI firm. And, because the two had been so private with the cases they assisted with several years ago, no one had ever really dealt with Mika. He was the silent partner. Even Barry hadn't known who Mika was.

Together, James and Mika decided that the best way to

protect me was for Mika to score the modeling slot that came up following Alec's untimely death. What neither of them had planned on was for Mika to fall for me in the process of the investigation.

Addison discovered that Barry had been guilty all along when she put her own plan into play. She'd written an article that basically made the police department look incredibly juvenile — a national laughingstock. When she met with the new Captain and threatened to run it, he claimed to have no idea what she was talking about. In truth, he didn't. As far as he knew, I was simply off the grid, not accepting assignments. Barry had even kept the Captain and my dad from speaking, a task to be sure. The one thing Addison and the Captain realized their stories had in common was Barry and that's when everything else began falling into place.

"Doing okay?" Addison asked me, checking my mug, which I'd hardly sipped.

"Yes," I said as I handed her the mug. "I can't have any more tea though. I'll float away."

She clucked like a mother hen, but took the mug from my hands and strode towards the kitchen. "Can I make you something to eat?"

"Not hungry," I responded.

"You should eat something," Mika encouraged.

"Not if she doesn't feel like it," James responded gently.

"Okay!" I said, forming my hands in a T for timeout. "What I feel like is having everyone go home."

The room drew quiet. "You can't be serious," Addison said.

"Look," I said with a sigh. "I appreciate what everyone here has done."

"But?" Rory asked me.

"But Barry was caught." I shrugged. "He's spending the night in prison."

"Your door is currently a toothpick," Addison pointed out. It was true. The police had more or less destroyed my front door when they broke in following the sniper shot. The door hung loosely from the top hinge and swung back and forth, squeaking slightly when anyone so much as looked at it.

I sighed. "I'll just drape a curtain over it until management gets here."

"You can stay with us," Rory offered. Clearly he meant himself and Addison. It was still weird that they were a couple. They were just so — different. From the looks on James's and Mika's faces, I could tell that they thought the same thing.

"I appreciate that, but I want to stay here," I told him, curling my feet under my body.

Mika began to speak, but I put my hand over his mouth. "Alone," I said, meeting his gaze. "Please."

The four of them looked at one another warily but eventually began to gather their things, slowly making their way to the door. Addison and Rory walked out first, Addison shooting me a worried puppy-eyed face as Rory practically dragged her to the elevator. James followed after them, with Mika hot on his heels.

Once everyone had gone, I took a lightweight dark-colored sheet and draped it across my front door. I'd already contacted my landlord to tell him what had happened. While he seemed incredibly skeptical of my story, he'd promised to get everything replaced as soon as possible. In this building that meant, "I'll get to it when I get to it." I thanked my lucky stars that my killer was off the streets.

Later, when I was curled up on the couch, my gun beside me, tucked loosely behind a pillow, a Hershey bar in one hand and a glass of white wine in the other, there was a light knock on the wall outside of my front "door." "Come in," I called, not really caring who it was as I eyed my weapon. I still didn't have a clue how to shoot it, but I didn't think that, that would really matter to whomever saw it.

I heard two sets of footsteps and felt my heart rate pick up ever so slightly. Dropping my candy bar, I went to reach for my gun. When I looked up, however, it was none other than James and Mika. "I thought I told you both to go home," I joked good-naturedly, willing my racing heart to slow. Like that was even possible now. "And despite what you may have heard, I am not that kind of girl." They both smiled but said nothing. I decided to draw it out of them. "What can I do for you?"

They eyed each other nervously in a "you go," "no, you go," sort of way. Finally, Mika cleared his throat. "We both like you," he told me.

"But you were friends first," I answered. "I get it." It wasn't like I imagined either of them having interest in me in the first place. No harm, no foul. Hearing it was really just going to ruin my night. Because, you know, being held at gunpoint in your own apartment didn't damper an evening or anything.

"We are friends," James supplied. "However, we were wondering how you felt about dating."

I was quiet for a few seconds while that question sank in. "Dating?" I squeaked.

"Yes," Mika responded. "Both of us."

I looked from one to the other, then back to the first. Was I hallucinating? Had I been dropped in the middle of a dream? Perhaps I really was dead and had just imagined the whole entire rescue. "Have you both thought about this? Reasonably?"

"Yes," they answered in unison.

For a moment I was speechless. When I pinched myself and felt it, I knew I was living reality. "I'm not a competition," I told them, unsure. "If anyone gets screwed over in this scenario, I don't want it to be me."

"I think that, that's something we have in common," Mika answered with a smile, looking to James.

I nodded, thoughtful. "Can I think about it?"

The two looked at each other. This clearly wasn't the

answer they'd expected, but they shrugged. I took a moment of pleasure from being able to restrain myself. "Sure. Just let us know what you decide," James told me.

"Goodnight," Mika added, walking towards the door.

"Goodnight," I said to them with a little wave.

They disappeared behind the sheet and I heard their steps echoing down the hallway to the stairwell. Taking a bite from my Hershey bar and slugging it down with a sip of wine, I zoned out watching the television for all of 30 seconds before I threw off my blankets and went barreling down the hallway in my flannel pajamas and pig slippers. I didn't even care how crazy I looked in that moment. You wouldn't have either. Trust me.

"Wait!" I cried, just as the door to the stairwell slammed shut. It reopened quickly and the two men poked their heads around it to look at me in anticipation. My heart pattered slightly faster as I took in just how attractive they both were. I truly didn't understand where my sudden stroke of luck had come from, but I wasn't about to let it slip past.

"I've thought about it," I told them with a devilish grin. "Who is free tomorrow night?"

THE END

Allison Janda is a writer with New York Times bestseller dreams. She currently resides in Nebraska with her two dogs, one of which acts more like a cat.

Visit her today (or tomorrow, if you're in a hurry right now) at:

AllisonJanda.com
Twitter: @AllisonJanda
Facebook.com/AllisonJJanda

39349182R00146

Made in the USA
Middletown, DE
16 March 2019